THE YEAR THE GYPSIES CAME

THE YEAR the GYPSIES CAME

Linzi Glass

HENRY HOLT AND COMPANY

NEW YORK

This is a work of fiction. Names, characters, places, and incidents are either the product of the author's imagination or are used fictitiously, and any resemblance to actual persons, living or dead, business establishments, events, or locales is entirely coincidental.

The author wishes to acknowledge the following references:
Long Walk to Freedom: The Autobiography of Nelson Mandela. Published by Little, Brown and Company, 1994.
The Social System of the Zulus, by Eileen Jensen Krige. Published by Shuter and Shooter (Pietermaritzburg, South Africa), 1950; 7th edition, 1977.
When Lion Could Fly and Other Tales from Africa, told by Nick Greaves, illustrated by Rod Clement. Published by Barron's, 1993.
Zulu Fireside Tales: A Collection of Ancient Zulu Tales to Be Read by Young and Old Alike, edited by Phyllis Savory, illustrated by Sylvia Baxter. Published by Carol Publishing Group, 1993.

Henry Holt and Company, LLC, *Publishers since 1866*
175 Fifth Avenue, New York, New York 10010
www.henryholtchildrensbooks.com

Henry Holt® is a registered trademark of Henry Holt and Company, LLC.
Copyright © 2006 by Linzi Alex Glass
All rights reserved. Distributed in Canada by H. B. Fenn and Company Ltd.

Library of Congress Cataloging-in-Publication Data
Glass, Linzi Alex.
The year the gypsies came / Linzi Alex Glass—1st ed.
p.   cm.
   Summary: In Johannesburg, South Africa, in the late 1960s, twelve-year-old Emily, who longs for affection from her quarreling parents, finds comfort in the stories of a Zulu servant and in her friendship with a young houseguest who has an equally troubled family.
ISBN-13: 978-0-8050-7999-9
ISBN-10: 0-8050-7999-8
[1. Family problems—Fiction.   2. Johannesburg (South Africa)—History—20th century—Fiction.
3. South Africa—History—1961—Fiction.   4. Apartheid—Fiction.] I. Title.
PZ7.G481237Ye2006   [Fic]—dc22   2005050314

First Edition—2006

Designed by Laurent Linn / Spot art by Peter MacKennan

Printed in the United States of America on acid-free paper. ∞

10   9   8   7   6   5   4   3   2   1

For my extraordinary daughter, Jordan, the song of my soul,
and my father, Harold, whose kindness knows no bounds

Last night the gypsies came—
Nobody knows from where.
Where they've gone to nobody knows,
And nobody seems to care!

—FROM "GYPSIES" BY RACHEL FIELD

Author's Note

There was, when I was growing up, an old Zulu night watchman at whose feet I would sit and listen, wide-eyed, while he told me stories of his people from long ago.

In telling Buza's stories, I have taken the old night watchman's tales, told so caringly to me, and have rewritten and embellished them with various other versions of similar stories told throughout Africa that I have since heard and read.

For the benefit of the reader, I have added a list of the Afrikaans and Zulu words used that I hope add to the enjoyment of the story.

Prologue

My family was, in a way, not unlike the city in which we lived. Johannesburg, called *iGoli* in Zulu—the "golden one." A city surrounded for nearly a hundred miles by colossal piles of gray rock and fine yellow sand. Man-made mountains so dramatic in their shape that they resemble giant chopped-off pyramids towering over the city. Like some fabulous creation of a forgotten civilization rather than the work of sweaty gold miners burrowing like moles deep within the earth to get at the hidden treasure.

Spectacular and magical, these mammoth monuments glisten over the city. But if you should feel compelled to look closer at them, to touch their shimmering forms, you will find, as you approach, that the particles blowing off them sting your cheeks. And when you reach to touch them, to hold a cluster of the gold in your hand, it will crumble and run through your fingers like sand. For the illusion of a family held together as ours was is not unlike a mine dump. It is just dust.

We lived, my parents, my fifteen-year-old sister, Sarah, and I, not quite thirteen, at 99 Winslow Lane, a great, old rambling house that sat on two acres of wild and abundant garden in an older neighborhood of Johannesburg. Winslow Lane was a street of curves and bends. Dark curves, where the homes, set against lush foliage, spoke of stillness and soft air. A road with houses on one side and blue gum woods on the other. Beyond the woods was Zebra Lake, named because of its closeness to the city zoo, which stood on the far side of the murky water. It was not unusual for me to fall asleep with the faint roar of a lion or the laugh of a hyena coming across the lake in the quiet of the night, transporting me in dreams to a tent in the most uninhabited part of the bush. For our house, while firmly planted in suburbia, stood on the edge of the wild.

In those early years, my parents used a powerful formula that kept our family together. As soon as the tension between them became unbearable, they would invite a houseguest to come and stay with us. As if by magic, the presence of the new arrival eased the strain between them, and for as long as there was an outsider living with us, the dust of their discontent would briefly settle, and our house would seem to shimmer.

When I was nine, Paul, a radical student with a terrible stammer, stayed with us for a whole summer. He lived in our outside rumpus room, which he painted in psychedelic swirls of orange and purple—the look of the early sixties—and where from under his door often came the sweet scent of burning incense. I once ventured uninvited into Paul's room after school, and there, to my amazement, sitting on top of him, stark naked, was his girlfriend, MoonRay. "Wh . . . wh . . . wh . . ."

was all he managed to get out before I slammed the door shut and fled.

When I described what I had seen to Sarah, she blushed deeply and told me that what Paul was probably doing was, "probably push-ups, Emily, probably push-ups."

Paul was followed by Rocco, a moody artist who was dating Anthea, a divorced friend of my mother's. Rocco lived in our garage, where he sculpted abstract figures from pieces of old scrap metal. He and Anthea would have loud, passionate fights that invariably ended up with one of them storming off into the woods. Rocco's relationship with Mother's friend lasted less than a year, and he moved out of our garage once they broke up.

Several less interesting houseguests followed. But in the spring of 1966, there was no one living with us, and the tension between my parents was left to germinate and grow like untended weeds: in the bedrooms, in the kitchen, in the dark spaces behind the curtains, and in the hallway closets. It was then that the gypsies came.

Were it not for our proximity to the lake and the woods where they were camped, we might never have encountered them. It was from beyond the lake that they came into our lives. From where, I do not know; no one ever asked. It did not seem to matter at the time. They simply walked into our world from across the road. Weary travelers carrying the fates of our lives in their dank pockets.

But our gypsies were not black-eyed girls in scarlet shawls

with silver loops through their ears. There was no shaggy dog, no swarthy men with handkerchiefs around their necks dancing wildly in the moonlight. They were a family of four. Wanderers, without roots, without course or direction, nomads, lost in a suburban wilderness. Yet for me they were, and always will be, gypsies. For they came to us that spring in a camping trailer and cast a spell over us, and changed our lives forever.

Beauty Time

Mother, Sarah, and I are in Mother's powder-blue bathroom. I think of it as Mother's bathroom and not Father's, even though he gets to use it too. Rows of her creams and lotions fill a small white cabinet that stands between the powder-blue washbasin and the powder-blue bathtub. Her set of electric curlers and five or six brushes of different shapes and sizes fill a basket on the porcelain back space of the toilet. Her silk robe hangs on a hook behind the bathroom door. Everything in this room is Mother's except for one small shelf that has Father's things on it. A bottle of Old Spice aftershave with what might be a pirate ship sailing across it, a ratty-looking shaving brush, and a can of shaving cream that's made a rusty brown ring underneath it. I've actually watched Father put the can back right over the ring, since Mother would be angry if she saw ugly marks in her bathroom.

Sarah's sitting on the toilet with the seat down, I'm in my scuffed-up shorts on the faded blue bathroom mat, and Mother, with wads of cotton stuck between her toes, has displayed herself on the edge of the bathtub. This is one of the few times lately that I get to have some of her attention, when Flaming Scarlet is drying on her nails. Mother's trapped for fifteen minutes like a bee in a hothouse, so she tells us stories from when she was young. These are her "nail-drying stories" that we only get to hear when we are invited to be stuck in the bathroom with her. They make her smile like the cat that ate the cream because mostly in her stories everyone comes out looking stupid, except herself.

I look up at Mother from my floor position. Her hair is glossy black, in the perfect latest style that flips at the ends, her mouth painted pink as bubblegum. Beautiful as always and "gussied up to the nines," as Father likes to say. I try long and hard to imagine that she once was, according to her, a tomboy just like me when she was my age. It makes me feel joined to her in a special kind of way, like I'll grow up pretty, just the way she says she did by the time she was fifteen, the age Sarah is now; except Mother was the most popular and one of the richest girls at school, and Sarah isn't all those things. Sarah's pretty all right, but we aren't super-rich with private drivers and crystal glasses at every meal like Mother used to have. Mother says manners are what matter most and that she could eat perfectly with real silver knives and forks by the time she was three. No true tomboy would ever eat with silver cutlery is what I believe.

Mother starts her story, her eyes moving back and forth from her nails to Sarah's pretty cheeks and hair. Sarah's hair is washed and shiny; the red color glows like fire around her face with flames falling loose onto her pale shoulders. She's sitting there so sparkly and bright, and me, I'm just a dark-haired pile on the floor that could easily be missed. Mother's eyes keep being pulled in Sarah's direction, and I feel a big lump starting in my throat like a piece of rough crust's got stuck there. If Sarah knew how badly I was hurting for Mother to look down at me just now and then, she'd come over and hug me and call me "silly billy."

"Mama and Papa Joe refused to let me go overseas with Delia Gordon when I was seventeen," Mother says, blowing frosted breath onto her hands. "You've met her, girls, tall and kind of beaky looking."

"Yes, Mother." Sarah sucks on a piece of her long red hair while I twirl bits of straggly blue rug thread around my finger and try to swallow the stuck-crust feeling out of my throat.

Mother waves her hands in the air so her nails dry faster. "Well, Delia's family was fantastically rich, richer than Papa Joe was, even though Papa Joe had a Bentley—that's a fancy car, girls."

"We know that, Mother." Sarah rolls her eyes, then smiles sweetly at Mother so as not to get her going on the fact that it's not ladylike to roll your eyes.

"Well, Delia wanted me to go with her for a month all over Europe. She was, poor thing, no great beauty, and thought having me with her on the trip would help attract the fine men of Europe into our company. Well, horror of horrors! Mama and Papa Joe flat-out refused, no matter how much I begged.

Even Papa for once wouldn't budge. They had already planned a European family vacation with me."

Mother paces around the bathroom as she talks. Sarah's brushing her hair, and I've given up looking up at Mother like a sick puppy and started searching in the medicine cabinet for a Band-Aid for my scratched tree-climbing elbow.

"Girls, listen, this is good," Mother says impatiently, waving us to sit down, nail polish fumes hitting me in the face and making me woozy for a second. Sarah and I take our seats with our backs against the bathroom door. The curtain's about to go up and Mother's standing center stage, green eyes flashing like GO signs.

"Only ten more minutes till her nails are dry. I've got masses of homework to do," Sarah whispers to me, resting her head on her knees.

"Well, I was burning mad, you can only imagine. Papa went to his study and Mama went back to the sitting room to knit— I remember she was knitting a red sweater for her miniature schnauzer, Harriet—God, I hated that dog; anyway, I was so upset that I decided to run a bath to calm my nerves. I poured loads of mint-green bubble bath into the water, then went to my bedroom to change. Problem was, I felt so darn upset, girls, that I lay down and fell asleep on the bed."

Mother sits on the edge of the bathtub and taps her ostrich fluffball slipper up and down and blows hard on her nails.

"Well, girls"—sparks in her eyes as she holds Sarah's gaze— "can you guess what happened?"

"The bath overflowed," I say eagerly, like I'm supposed to win a prize or something.

"Right!" she says, looking for an instant at me, pleased as Punch and snapping her fingers so quick and sharp, like a gun popping. "The bathwater ran *all* the way from upstairs down the twenty-five cream carpeted stairs—remember the water was now green, girls—past Mama in her sitting room and right under the door of Papa's oak-paneled study."

"Oh, boy!" I say. "You must have got into so much trouble."

"Oh, they were angry, they were hopping mad!" Mother touches her hair with her palms like she's checking to see if it's still in place. "But they let me go to Europe with Delia."

"They did?" I say.

"See, it made sense in the end. Why, half the house looked like a moldy green swamp, and it would take about a month to repair. Mama and Papa decided it was better if I wasn't there, what with all those workmen about whistling and leering at me."

Mother seems happy for a second, then notices Sarah. The party's over. "Sarah, get your hair out of your mouth. That's disgusting! Fifteen and still sucking like a baby. What would a nice boy want with a girl who uses her hair as a pacifier?" She points hot Flaming Scarlet fingers at Sarah, who spits out her hair in what might be mistaken for Mother's direction.

Mother's always telling Sarah what boys want and don't want. She says they don't like a girl telling them what to do in a firm, tough-sounding voice. Mother says that Sarah should tell a boy what she thinks he ought to do, but she should use a real soft voice on him and always make the boy feel whatever you tell him was his idea and not your own. Mother must have different rules for girls once they get married because lots of times she raises her voice harshly at Father, telling him that he doesn't make enough money and what she thinks he should do in his chocolate business like they're her very important ideas and she knows best.

The other day, when Mother was lazing on her bed with cucumber slices on her eyelids, in a deep and earnest conversation with her lah-de-dah friend Anthea on the phone, I overheard everything she said. She didn't know I was in the room, on account of the cucumber slices. She told Anthea that Sarah, with her brains and beauty, would not be allowed to make the same mistake that she did and marry the wrong man, who couldn't provide her with the lifestyle she was used to. "Not if I have anything to do with it, she won't," Mother fumed.

And me? I wondered as I sat crouched quietly on the side of the bed. What about me? Then as if she had read my mind Mother continued, "Emily," she sighed, "Emily marches to a beat of her own. She's different. I daresay I haven't quite figured out what that beat is." Mother sighed again, patting the cucumber slices back into position.

I wanted to jump up from my hiding place and go and take those cucumber slices off her eyes and tell her that I would dance to any beat she wanted if only she would tell me which exact beat it was.

Mother can be sweet sometimes, especially to Sarah, and

sometimes to me too. When she is, it feels like her friendly moods are going to last forever, but then suddenly it's over, like at the end of a good movie when the lights have gone on and you have to get yourself out of that other place, where everything felt better and unreal.

Sarah gets up off the bathroom floor. She sets her shoulders back and fixes her eyes straight ahead, like a page boy, then quietly closes the bathroom door behind her. Sarah tries to avoid Mother's up-and-down moods. She'd rather go to her room and read a book than slam doors and make a big show. Sarah's pure and good like clear water, while Mother's like thick oil, hard to look through. When you put both ingredients in a jar, it's the oil that always rises to the top. I guess Sarah knows that.

"Sarah's got to remember she's a young lady and not a child anymore!" Mother says, ripping the cotton out from between her toes.

I'm still sitting on the bathroom mat where I've made a blue-thread face with a sad half-circle mouth on the tile floor.

"I have a headache," Mother says, looking down at me. "I'm going to lie down. Pick up the stuff, Emily, okay?"

She leaves me with the sad blue-thread face and the pieces of cotton from her toes tossed all over the floor like bits of confetti after a parade, and patters out the bathroom in her silly toeless slippers.

While I'm cleaning up, I wonder about the story of Mother and her trip to Europe. About how much of it happened exactly the way she says. But both Mother's parents, who were quite old when they had her, were dead by the time I was born, so I can't check with them. I remember once hearing Father yell at Mother, "Don't try one of your manipulative bathwater tricks on me, Lil. It may have worked with your parents, but it won't work with me!" when she wanted to go away to the beach in Cape Town with another one of her fancy friends.

After I'm done in the bathroom, I go to Father's study, where books with maroon bindings and gold writing lie dusty and unread on the shelves. These are books that Father says he's mostly kept from his college days. There are even some that he's had from when he was a boy. *Huckleberry Finn, The Hardy Boys,* and lots of stuffy books about Roman-Dutch law. I think Father was planning on becoming a lawyer, but when he failed the exams he went into one of Papa Joe's businesses instead.

I find a dictionary that's new-looking and not dusty sticking out between the old books and look up the word *manipulative.* It means "someone who manages and controls cleverly." I place one of the used-up cotton balls that I spy lost in the cuff of my shorts inside the book and mark the place of the word.

Outside Father's study window two African hoopoes peck with their curved beaks for beetles in the bushes. One hoopoe is smaller and dull brown, and the other has a bright reddish crown. I wonder about beauty in the bird world, how it's always the male who's got the prettier feathers. Mother probably wouldn't have been too happy being a female bird. I sometimes think she married Father at nineteen because his last name was Iris, and by marrying him she became a double flower, Lily Iris. Mother likes things that look and sound pretty.

I'm still in Father's study when I hear him come in through the front door. The tired slapping of his briefcase against his leg, then a thud as he drops it onto the pinewood living room floor. Father smokes a lot and seems worried a good deal about things that I can't see or hear. He spends hours in his study going through papers that have to do with his imported chocolate business.

Father comes from Witbank, a small coal-mining town about a hundred miles from Johannesburg. Sometimes I'll catch him looking up from his papers and, if he's in the mood, I might get him to tell me a thing or two about being a boy in Witbank. His eyes always look past me when he talks about the faded yellow kitchen where his mother baked him apricot jam turnovers.

There's this picture of Father on the side table next to the *riempie* stool in the living room. He's maybe sixteen and is standing behind the dusty counter in his family's mining supply store. Father had lots of curly dark hair then, but his eyes had the same clear and kind of surprised look to them. On the shelves behind him you can see packets of Impala *mielie meal,* cans of Nestlé's condensed milk, and long strips of *biltong* hanging from hooks.

He left Witbank to go to university in Johannesburg soon

after his mother died and hardly ever visited home again once he met Mother there. Mother didn't like Witbank. She said it smelled bad from the mines, and the black soot made her skin look dull.

I've often tried to imagine Witbank and the miners and the soot and the mining store, but I can't. Father has never taken us there. All I can come up with is a place where everything smells very bad or everything smells wonderful, like hot, freshly baked jam turnovers.

"Emily," Father says as I walk past him on my way to Lettie, our nanny, who is cooking dinner in the kitchen, "I have a new chocolate for you to taste. Just came in from the factory in Belgium. Almond-cream soft centers. They're quite delicious, actually." He holds a neatly wrapped dark-brown chocolate out toward me. I'm about to unwrap it, even though I'm sure I'll like it about as much as I like all his bitter-tasting imported chocolates, when Mother glides by.

"Honestly, Bob. It's almost dinnertime. Don't you ever think? She doesn't need all that sugar, and besides it's bad for her skin." She flashes eyes like a cat who's about to pounce at him.

Father sighs, looks over from me to her, and stuffs the chocolate into his jacket pocket.

"Tell Lettie to bring my dinner to me in my study," he says curtly to Mother. "Frankly, I don't need to come home to be instantly attacked every night." He marches past me and mumbles, "Sorry, Emmie, I'm too worn out to take on the likes of your mother right now." He hands me the chocolate from his pocket. "Taste it later, or whenever you please." He turns to Mother and shoots her a hard glare, then leaves.

I feel the chocolate, soft and crumbling, already melting from the heat of his hand. And I feel myself crumbling too, little pieces you can't see that break off on the inside.

Later, even though their bedroom door is closed, the yelling wakes me in the dead of night. It's twenty-two steps from my room to theirs. Fifteen steps from my room to Sarah's. Sarah's room is closer to them, so she gets to hear their yelling even louder than I can.

The fights always start with something as small as chocolates and then become something else, something bigger. I can't hear the actual words, just the sounds of anger. It comes at me from under their door and slams into me so hard that it takes my dreams away. Then, when it gets too loud in my head, I go to Sarah. I tiptoe softly, like a mouse that leaves no footprints on the carpet. Creep into her room that's perfect as a picture book. Everything has its place. Pencils lined up straight on her desk, shoes in neat matching rows in the closet.

I stand at the foot of her bed. Sarah's long red hair, shining like a glowworm in the dark, is the only part of her I can see. She's already awake.

"Don't worry, Em, it'll soon stop. It always does," Sarah says to me, but her voice sounds far off, like an echo that comes from an empty space—a place inside her where the door's already been shut. She gets out of bed in her ghost-white nightgown and takes me by the hand and brings me back to lie next to her in a warm spot.

"It's safe in here, Em," she whispers as she climbs in beside me. "The mess out there can't reach us in here, can't reach us at all," she murmurs in a sleepy voice.

I stay very still, keep my body so tight, try to stop the sounds that reach into me through the cracks. Close my eye-holes and cover my ear-spaces with a pillow, until the loud noises that come at me stop.

Late Afternoon

Late Afternoon

I bend to talk to the jacaranda buds that were silly enough to have left their branches in search of instant adventure and now lie quiet and still on our gravel driveway. They look rumpled and sad, so I whisper to them that they are a magical purple carpet and that later, when it's dark and everyone's asleep, we'll fly away to some far-off place together. This, I decide, cheers them up considerably, so I hop painfully from one bare foot to the other, in my shorts and half-muddy school shirt, down the driveway, careful not to step on my purple friends. It's not a good idea to be barefoot on gravel, with points that bite into the undersides of your feet like fish with teeth. I won't hurt the buds though; they've had enough upsets for one day.

At the bottom of the garden is Buza, our old Zulu night watchman. He sits on his wooden stool and threads colored beads onto cut pieces of new copper wire that he unravels from a big shiny roll beside him.

"*Hai wena*, Miss Emily," Buza says as I plunk myself down next to him and rub my feet. "This old Zulu cannot see too good anymore. *Ay*, it hurts my head." He touches his watery eyes with a wrinkled brown hand and puts the half-finished bracelet on the ground next to me.

Even before I was born, Buza was there at the bottom of the garden. He came with Mother when she left her parents' house to marry Father and moved to Winslow Lane. Mother would not think of "living in that ugly big house, with that frightening forest across the road," unless Buza came with her to guard the gates.

Buza's job is to sit all night on his stool and watch the street and the dark woods and listen for someone or something. He has a knobbly stick always at his side. His grandfather cut it from the branch of a mopane tree that was chopped down in Natal and gave the stick to Buza when he was seventeen. This is what protects us all from danger. Buza tells me he's never needed anything else because the stick has the power of sixty dead Zulu warriors inside it.

Buza isn't like anyone else I know. It doesn't matter if he is quiet or busy threading beads or rolling his stick between his hands, he always listens to what I have to say, and when he looks at me, he looks deep at me, like he's seeing every scratch on my knee and every mark on my face. He looks down at me that way now as I sit beside him.

"You look to me like you need a story to put into your head, Miss Emily. There is too much frowning on your face today."

"Tell me warrior stories, Buza. War and fighting stories."

"Ay, I have forgotten those. I am tired from the stories of

great Zulu wars. We fought too many battles. Too much, too much."

Buza looks at me with soft brown eyes that remind me of the milky cocoa that Lettie gives me before I go to bed at night. His hair is curly gray and his earlobes are stretched long and have shiny blue and orange corks stuck through them. I think how good it would be if Miss Erasmus, my history teacher, could see him, with his gentle eyes and kind voice. At school the pictures in our history books have Zulu warriors with angry painted faces and sharp *assegais* in their hands.

Last week in class, Miss Erasmus told us, "During the Great Trek, our brave Afrikaners killed thousands of Zulu warriors on the banks of the Ncome River as they trekked north in their ox wagons." She peered down at us over her short, rubbery snout, then lifted it upward and sniffed the air hard a few times, as if she could smell the sweat of a Zulu in the classroom. When she was satisfied that there was no dangerous black man around, she carried on. "Wave after wave of Zulus kept coming until the Ncome ran thick and red with their blood. That is why it is called the Battle of Blood River," she said, holding on to the history book tight against her chest like it was the Bible.

While I listened to her squeaky voice, I could see the Afrikaners kneeling with barrels of gunpowder behind their circle of ox wagons. They had names like Pietrus and Martienus and wore floppy felt hats and were shooting at men with shiny earlobes like Buza. I imagined the Zulu warriors' *assegais* floating downstream, the spearheads red from their blood, their beaded necklaces and bracelets lying like buried treasure at the bottom of the river.

"What are you thinking about, Miss Emily? You are too serious today," Buza says, picking up the beads and starting to string again.

"I want to take you with me to school one day."

"*Ayzirorie!* You are a strange one today."

"Strange is how I feel." I dig my heels back into the ground. "Buza, did you ever feel like your inside and your outside don't fit together? Like they're separate?" I ask softly.

Buza makes a low clicking sound with his tongue.

I think how angry Father would be if he knew I was talking to Buza about these things inside me. The servants, Father always says, should not know more than they need to know. He says that while they are kind, good people, they aren't family and that there's always the possibility of them leaving and going to work for another family. Father insists that what goes on in our lives is private and is best not discussed with them. But Lettie spoon-fed me porridge and carried me on her back when I was a baby, and Buza taught me to tell the time and knows how I'm feeling without me ever having to say a word. There is nothing I won't tell Buza, but there are lots of things I won't tell Father.

"I can't sleep well. Mother and Father argue too much at night. I break into lots of pieces when they yell so loud," I say to Buza.

"*Hayakona!*" Buza shakes his head sadly. "This is not good. Madam Lily and Master Bob, they must work this *indaba* out.

Come, let me tell you a story, and you can help me put the green beads here and here," he says, pointing to the bracelet.

He begins, slow and soft like a lullaby, note by note strung like the beads, one at a time.

"Once, Miss Emily, in the land there was a great drought. For a long, long time no rain had fallen. The earth, it was hard, and the cornfields dried up. There was, Miss Emily, living in a small village, where hunger was the only thing on people's minds, a young girl called Ma-we. It happened one morning that her father told Ma-we and her brother to go to the place where the guinea fowl sat on its eggs. 'Guard it well,' said the father. 'Keep away the hyenas. Your mother and I are going to look for food in the town.'

"Ma-we and her brother watched, throwing stones at the hyenas that came there, and when the sun was hot and high above, they became very thirsty. The children did not want to disobey their father, but the heat was so strong that they began to feel weak. 'We will go,' Ma-we said, 'to the water hole there by the great cave, and when we have drunk, we can return very quickly.'"

"Oh, no, they left the eggs, Buza!" I reach up and take more beads from his wrinkled palm.

"Yes, listen, Miss Emily. It was too hot, and they were very thirsty. And when they come back, they see that a big hyena has come out from the bushes. It has eaten the guinea fowl, and all the eggs are broken into many pieces. *Hai wena!*"

Buza puts the half-finished bracelet on his knee and reaches into a pouch that he carries on a string around his waist. He takes out a small silver tin of black snuff and pours some into his hand and puts a pinch of it up into his nose.

"Power medicine." He smiles at me and sneezes loudly twice. "To keep my head clear and strong." He smacks his hands together like cymbals, to dust the snuff off them. "Well, Ma-we and her brother were very much afraid, and Ma-we picked up very carefully all the small pieces of the broken shells and put the pieces in her apron. And she cry out, 'Who will help me? Who will help me fix these?'

"Now, Ma-we, she is a blessed one, and she hear the cry of a bird, *pirr-pirr, pirr-pirr.* And she look down and she sees the *i-Nsedhlu* bird, the honeyguide bird, its wings caught in the thorn bush. *Pirr-pirr,* it cries. And Ma-we, she bends down and with her hands she frees the honeyguide bird from the thorns. The small bird, it is so happy and it flies up, and it sings *whit-pirr, whit-pirr,* and it calls to Ma-we, 'Because you have been so kind to me, now I will help you. Come, follow me.'

"Now, Ma-we and her brother, they heard their parents coming, and they were very much afraid, so they ran down and they follow the honeyguide bird to the deep cave. And Ma-we said, 'Let us go into the cave, and then we can enter the Land of the Spirits together.'

"But her brother, he was too frightened and did not follow Ma-we, and he went back to his parents, and he say, 'My sister, she is gone.'

"The parents, they ran quick to the deep cave. And the

mother, she cry, 'Ma-we, Ma-we, I have no anger for you. Come back! Come back, my daughter!' But Ma-we has gone already into the Spirit Land."

"Is she dead, Buza?"

"Wait, wait, listen nicely, Miss Emily. Inside the cave, the honeyguide shows Ma-we the nest of wild bees. And the honeyguide, he shows her with his beak how to use the beeswax to fix the broken shells together and to put honey into the eggs. And she makes the eggs whole again and full of honey, but having lots of joinings."

Buza reaches down and takes my elbow and wrist and pushes them toward each other. "Like so," he says. "Like Ma-we's egg, *mnta-na-mi.*"

My skin, where Buza has touched, feels warm.

"Listen good, Miss Emily. Ma-we knows how to glue broken things with the wax of wild bees and how to fill it with sweet honey."

"What happened then?" The beads glow green in my hand.

"Now, when all the broken eggs were fixed and full with honey, the honeyguide bird say to Ma-we, 'Now you must return to your parents, and with all these eggs, your family will have much to eat, *whit-pirr, whit-pirr.*' And Ma-we, she goes with the honeyguide, and when they come to the entrance of the cave, they stop. 'Here,' the bird says, and it lays a very tiny egg into Ma-we's hand."

"The honeyguide bird's own egg, Buza?"

"Yes, Miss Emily. It is so small and very light in color. So very small that if you sneezed too hard it might be blown all the way to Soweto township." Buza holds his fingers less than an inch apart in front of me. He pretends to throw the imaginary egg up in the air, a look of surprise on his face as it travels away from him then lands back into his palm. Buza and I laugh at his game before he carries on with the story.

"Then, Miss Emily, the honeyguide says, 'Remember the egg—make it whole and you will always be happy, for inside it is full of sweetness.'

"And Ma-we went out of the cave and ran back to her family's hut, and they were very much pleased to see her. Then the village people filled their bellies with the richness of all the honey-filled eggs that Ma-we had fixed, and, Miss Emily, like magic, the honey-filled eggs fed them all until the drought was over.

"And for all her life, Ma-we lived in happiness. And she kept the honeyguide's tiny egg close to her heart, and she always remembered what the honeyguide had told her: 'Make the egg whole, for there is sweetness inside. *Whit-pirr, whit-pirr.*'

"*Kunjalo!* I have said so!"

Buza and I sit quietly in the shadow of the story for a few minutes. His story is like a person who has just left us after a short visit. Ma-we, so real, sitting next to me on the grass. I am not ready to let her go.

Buza looks down at me, eyes so brown. "No sweetness in a broken child, no sweetness in a family with so much cracks."

"Maybe the wax of wild bees would help."

Buza laughs. "Ay, Miss Emily, you are too smart, too smart."

The story is finished, and the bracelet is complete in his hands. Buza holds it toward me, then puts it on my wrist. It warms me all over, like I'm glued together with honey.

Saturday

Mother, Sarah, and I are having tea on the front lawn.

There is so much prettiness around us. Soft, cushiony green grass cut evenly that rolls out for yards and yards in front of us like a flat ocean. On one of its borders is a row of pink blossom trees, while sweet-smelling jasmine falls like white sleet along the length of the far wall. Ahead, at the bottom of the garden, is a big oak tree, its giant branches making huge finger-like shadows across the lawn, and along the driveway toward the gates sway the jacaranda trees, dropping their adventurous purple buds every time the wind puffs up. But none of this prettiness matters because the meanest of words were just said between Mother and Father before he stormed off into the woods. The angry sentences that they yelled at each other were like enormous scissors that cut away all the loveliness, all the trees and flowers, all the sweet-smelling jasmine, so that lying here on the lawn on the big mauve blanket that Lettie has laid down, halfheartedly playing a game of checkers with Sarah, I feel only dirt and dryness and dead leaves all around me.

I'm nearest to Mother, who leans back on her elbows, her

head tilted up toward the sun, her eyes closed like nothing in the world is bothering her, as if her fighting with Father in front of Sarah and me never happened.

"Scoot over would you, Emmie?" Mother nudges me over a bit with her red-painted toe. I see two hard lines between Mother's eyebrows starting to form and think of grapes that become shriveled-up raisins when they've been in the sun too long. Here's Mother with a wrinkled raisin face in a few years. A mixed-up giggle comes spilling out of me.

"What's funny, Emmie?" she murmurs, not moving.

"Nothing, just something tickled me from the grass. Your turn, Sarah."

Mother calls me Emmie when she feels bad about something, but I like the sound of it in her mouth, no matter the reason. Last night at dinner Father told Mother that she's only in a "fake" good mood if there are other people around. She got red-hot angry and said that he was being ridiculous, then she made a big show and aimed a forkful of mashed potatoes across the table at him, but never actually let it fly. I concentrated on cutting my chicken into tiny pieces for a long time until they were in perfect squares. Inside my head I kept screaming, "Can't you two just stop it? This is no family! Can't you act more like Mr. and Mrs. Wright?"

My only friend at school is Cynthia Wright. She doesn't care that I say dolls are boring and that pink is my least favorite color. She walks right up to the other girls in our class when they whisper about my short hair and tells them stuff like "don't judge a book by its cover" and reminds them about being nice to your fellow man that's written in the Bible that her mother reads to her every night.

Cynthia's father sometimes shows up for lunch when I'm over there. He and Cynthia's mother kiss hello at the door when he comes in, then her mother helps him off with his construction work boots before we can all sit down to eat the no-crust egg mayonnaise sandwiches and drink the lemonade that Mrs. Wright puts in front of us. Cynthia's mother always smiles and has on an apron and sits down last, after she's sure Mr. Wright is comfortable. Even though Cynthia always says she wishes she lived in a big house like I do, she doesn't know how lucky she is.

"Anyone for a scone and jam?" Mother asks, sitting up and spreading a napkin on her lap.

"Not yet. Game's too close," Sarah says quietly. She has on a striped lavender pinafore, and a few strands of her long red hair have spun themselves around the white buttons of her collar. In Sarah's eyes I see trapped tears that have spun themselves so tightly that they can't fall onto her cheeks but will fall instead back into the empty hollow place in her. I imagine a deep, dark well inside her that's filled with all the tears she never cries and how cold and damp she must feel under her pinafore and inside her kind, pale body.

While Mother lies sunning herself, we play quietly on the lawn. Sarah and I are extra gentle when we win checkers from each other. "Sorry, Em," "sorry, Sarah," we say each time we take a jump. I feel myself not wanting to have any of her checkers and would rather let her keep them all.

After a half hour or so, Mother stirs and sits herself up. She fans her flushed cheeks and gazes out into the woods.

"Your father's heading back already," she says, sounding disappointed and looking in the direction of the white pillars, where I see him, thin dark hair plastered back off his shiny forehead, walking at a fast pace through the gates, like an eagle on a mission.

"You're back much too soon, Bob," Mother says, eyes half-closed, her head turning away from him as he reaches us.

"Nastiness becomes you." Father breathes heavily over her.

"You're blocking my light, Bob."

"Nobody could ever block your light," Father snorts.

Sarah and I keep our eyes on the checkerboard between us. My eyes burn into the pieces. Red over black, black over red. Your jump. My jump. His jump. Her jump. Mother's jump. Father's jump. Jump. Jump. Jump. One jump after the other, all jumbled inside my head.

Neither one of them moves for a few painfully silent minutes, then Father slowly begins to circle the blanket we're sitting on.

"I have some news that might sweeten your sting, Lily," Father says, placing one hand on his hip as he walks. "*I met a traveler from an antique land—some gypsies.*" He stops and grins smugly down at Mother.

"Gypsies?" Mother raises an eyebrow, then squints up at

him from underneath the propped hand above her eyes. "How clever of you."

"Real gypsies?" Sarah sits up suddenly.

"Well, let's just say they're gypsies of a kind. Adventurers. Wanderers I met parked in their camping trailer in the woods." He lets out a breath, then takes a cigarette from his pocket and lights up. "I've invited them to stay with us for a while."

"Stay, Father? Where will they stay?" Sarah asks in a high-pitched voice, looking up at him wide-eyed.

"In their camping trailer on our property. Don't look so frightened, Sarah. They really seem awfully decent. A nice couple actually—"

"Do they have children?" I blurt out, while Sarah quietly lowers her eyes and flicks specks of grass off her pinafore.

"Yes, yes, two boys, I think they said." Father draws deeply on the cigarette and blows out a large smoke ring.

Mother is busy piling thick homemade strawberry jam and clotted cream onto a scone and acts like nothing's been said, like the only thing in the world that matters to her right now is the scone she's fixing.

"They arrived last night. Didn't know it's illegal to camp in the woods. They've been told they have to be out by nightfall," Father says, like he suddenly doesn't care who's listening and who's not.

"Are they staying long?" I ask, imagining a dark-haired gypsy couple in wild-colored scarves, a glowing fortune-telling ball between them, and two scruffy-looking boys with big sad eyes looking on while their parents read fortunes to strangers outside their trailer. The thought fills me with terror . . . and excitement.

"I told them we had a large garden and they could park their camping trailer in it for a while. Give them a chance to find somewhere to stay. They'll be here within the hour or so." Father blows two more smoke rings.

I watch them as they spin around one inside the other. There are no sounds, except for the sprinklers that hiss rainbow sprays into the quiet air. Sarah must notice the quiet too because she starts to tap a red checker against a black one. *Click, click, click,* like tap shoes on an empty stage.

Mother looks up from her scone. A small drop of strawberry jam clings to the side of her mouth. She looks directly at Father through the smoke rings that he keeps blowing. "Well, well, Bobby-boy. I didn't think you had it in you. What fun! Gypsy houseguests, how dee-vinely original! Do tell, what are they like? I'm all ears."

"You'll see for yourself, Lil. He's a robust sort of chap from the Australian outback. His wife seems interesting, I daresay quite unusual, actually. I'm quite sure he said they have two boys, but they didn't come out. Must have been inside the camping trailer."

Mother touches her sticky mouth and wipes away the strawberry jam with a lace napkin. We all watch her as she stands up and arches her back, stretching her arms high above her head. "Good!" she says. "We could all use some livening up around here. Don't look so glum, Sarah. No one's going to cast a spell on you, for goodness' sakes!" Mother laughs.

"That's settled, then. They can park over there." Father stamps his cigarette into the grass and points across the lawn to a spot near the driveway. Mother looks across at the same place.

I watch them standing apart but looking in the same direction and wonder if maybe they are both imagining the camping trailer that will soon be parked there. Something heavy seems to fall away between them. It makes me think of the big black rock I once saw on a school field trip to Pelindaba that rolled off a cliff and crashed onto the ground below. For a moment, I feel happy.

Arrival

Up the long driveway comes the tinny rattle of a Land Rover, the sound of loose pieces, like change rattling in a giant's pocket. It chokes its way up toward the house, spitting gravel in all directions. This is an injured car, I think, noticing the small metal chunks that hang from its sides. There is a dirty oil cloth tied to its bumper, its windows are covered with brown dust, and a wiper lies across its windshield like the crippled wing of a bird so I can't see the faces inside. Behind drags the camping trailer. Maybe it was once white or blue or red, but the paint has peeled in so many places that it's a dull gray now, except for the faded bumper stickers of places they've been that decorate its back end like rosettes.

We don't see too many Land Rovers in Johannesburg. They're mostly used in the bush. Once I saw one on a trip to the Kruger National Park. It was shiny olive green, speeding like a cheetah on the chase through the grasslands of the veld, keeping up with a herd of wildebeest, dust blowing everywhere from the tires and the hooves as they pounded across the plains of the bushveld.

The old Land Rover comes to a muttering stop on our driveway. I think how unlike the Land Rovers in the bush this one is, how here in the suburbs of Johannesburg it's a chained prisoner to the camping trailer, like a cheetah in the zoo.

It is late afternoon, and the shadows cover the woods and the driveway. They cover me and Sarah too, as we stand side by side and wait for the doors of the Land Rover to open.

I think of all the people who have lived with us before at different times and how used to outsiders Sarah and I have gotten and how things always seemed worse between Mother and Father after the guest left. This time, a whole family of people will be living with us—a strange gypsy family—and I wonder if maybe it takes not one houseguest, but a whole family to make my parents get along now.

I imagine a bonfire burning in our garden. Above it hangs a blackened pot where angry words are thrown in and boiled away, and shadowy gypsies give the brew to Mother and Father to drink so that they will be kind to each other.

My heart beats loud against my chest as the Land Rover door opens.

There comes first a man. A worn leather work boot kicking the door open. A big man with light brown hair and a smile for Sarah and me.

"G'day," he says. Creased khaki trousers that sag at the knees come toward us, "I'm Jock Mallory." Father was right, Jock is no real gypsy but looks more like a tanned cowboy. All thoughts of a gypsy brew vanish instantly.

"I'm Sarah, and this is Emily," Sarah says, sounding relieved by the tanned, healthy sight of him, and politely shakes his hand.

"Hey there, Em'ly." A rough, warm hand takes my hand for a second. "Where's the rest of my ragamuffin family?" Jock says, looking back toward the far side of the Land Rover.

The sound of crunching gravel. A cough. Someone spits on the ground.

Now a lady.

"This is my wife, Peg," Jock says.

Peg. It is not her I notice. It is the six-foot python that she wears peacefully wrapped around her neck, like some enormous necklace.

"Her name's Opalina," she says, showing chipped, jigsaw-puzzle teeth. Peg must have been pretty once, but her skin looks worn, stained by earth, rubbed through thin in places from years of use, like her husband's leather boots.

Opalina. Smooth, oily skin, clouds of black color on a milky-beige background, camouflaged as jewelry.

"I named her after the black opals of Lightning Ridge in Australia." She smiles. "You can touch her if you want. She won't bite." Peg leans toward me, a mixture of vanilla and the sweat of old clothes.

Opalina is inches from my face. I shake my head. I can't touch the snake. Not because I'm afraid, but because the snake seems like part of her body.

"Maybe later," I mumble and reach down and pick up a gray stone from the driveway.

"Where are your children?" Sarah asks, sounding cheery and unafraid, but I notice her keeping one eye on Opalina.

"Boys are a little bashful right now," Peg shrugs. Her voice is low and dry-sounding, like she could use a long drink of water.

Mother's face suddenly appears through the study window.

"Welcome," she calls, as if there are a hundred people standing in the garden. "I'll be out in a minute." Her hair is wrapped in a thick, pink towel, turban-style, and from here she looks soft and beautiful. Jock and Peg look toward the window and wave to her, like she's an Indian princess riding a fancy elephant.

"Wanna see inside and scare the bejeezus out of our boys?" Jock asks. "They've hardly ever seen girlies before."

Peg gives Jock a don't-tease-the-girls look. She tosses her blond stringy hair back and walks off toward Father, who is headed down the driveway with Lettie right behind him.

"Python's squeezed the sense of humor outta her." Jock laughs. "Only teasing about the boys. They're more or less okay, as far as boys go." He gives Sarah and me a curly-eyed wink. "C'mon ladies, let's go show them how pretty both of you are."

Jock pulls down the wobbly trailer steps, and Sarah and I follow him up. Jock has to duck his head as he passes under the door, and although Sarah and I fit through easily, I get a strange closed-in feeling, like I'm entering into a cave where there is little light, where maybe someone could get lost and never find her way out.

A peppery, damp smell hits me inside the camping trailer. Once my eyes get used to the half-light I see, at the far end of the room, a small stove with a copper kettle on it. Opposite, there's a mattress with a brown and orange bedspread, and against the far wall, on the other side, is a small partition where I can see the outline of a bunk bed.

"Streak, Otis, c'mon out and meet the girls." Silence. "You two are such ninny-boys. Do I have to come in there and wallop you both to get your hides moving?" Jock yells.

Shuffling feet. A large boy appears. His skin is red, like he's got a bad sunburn. He has a big forehead and dull blue eyes that are sunk deep in his head.

"Otis is sixteen." Jock looks back and forth from me to Sarah, as if he's worried about something.

"Hello, Otis," Sarah says kindly.

Otis takes a step forward, off-balance, like the drunk man I once saw in the street on New Year's Day. There are too many of us inside, and he trips and falls forward. He grabs for the nearest thing to hold on to, which happens to be Sarah's braids. Sarah lets out a shriek as she and Otis land in a messy heap on the floor. Otis laughs. A funny, high, ragged sound, like a mule braying. A mule with teeth like bad corn.

I have forgotten about the stone that I picked up outside until I feel its sharp edges digging into the soft flesh of my palm.

"Are you okay, girlie?" Jock bends over Sarah.

"Yes, fine. I'm fine." Sarah dusts herself off and gets to her feet. "It was just an accident." She looks over at Otis and pats him on the shoulder. "It's okay, really." Sarah's goodness seems to come out even more when there's an injured bird or person for her to fuss over.

"Dumb ox," a voice yells from inside the small room. A thin boy with golden colored skin and big dark eyes that can hardly be seen from under his messy mop of hair scowls out at us from the other room.

"Our other well-mannered son, Streak." Jock says "well-mannered" like he's reminding Streak in advance to watch his words.

"You don't look much like a girl." Streak points a dirty finger at me.

"Guess you didn't hear me, Streak. A tanning on that thick hide of yours is dessert for tonight." Jock's not smiling. He touches my short hair with the flat of his palm. "Streak's the other joker in this family. Don't take no notice."

Streak slips back through the door to the other room, where I see jumbled bedsheets and dirty clothes thrown about the floor.

"Where the hell's my chameleon, Otis?" Streak yells.

"Adunno. Adunno." Otis looks confused and scratches inside his pants.

Jock sighs and runs a big hand through his hair. "Sorry, girlies. They're a bunch of heathens. Never been to school, never lived in a house. My fault, see. I'm a wildlife photographer. Take pictures of big game for the magazines—sometimes. We're always on the go."

"Sounds like fun," Sarah says with a longing in her voice.

"In some ways it is, I guess." Jock whacks Otis on the head with the back of his hand. Otis is still scratching.

"It's okay. I've got the little bugger!" Streak shouts back.

He comes out from behind the door.

"Dare you to touch my chameleon." He looks over in my direction. "Here, take it." He holds the chameleon out to me and grins like a wicked imp. The chameleon is spotted green and pink, and its eyes and throat bulge out, but creatures like this don't scare me.

"Okay." I look at Streak level and unafraid as I hold my arm out. Streak puts the chameleon on it, and I force myself not to make a face or move a muscle as it fastens its claws onto my skin. Streak watches me closely, frowning at first, then he gives me a half-smile, as if I've passed some kind of test or something because I'm not squirming and carrying on the way most girls would with a scaly green creature attached firmly to their arm. I cock my head at him, then turn to hold the chameleon out in Sarah's direction.

"How funny it is." Sarah takes a dainty step back so as not to be to close to it. Streak and I give each other an even-eyed look.

"Yup. Funny, ugly thing." Otis smiles at Sarah.

"C'mon, ragamuffins, let's go find everyone," Jock says.

We leave the camping trailer in single file, like we do after school assembly on Fridays.

Outside there is still watery sunlight, and the chameleon digs its claws into my arm even deeper. I squint into the light and wonder if it's only me and the chameleon who notice how dark the camping trailer is inside.

Dinner

Dinner served at six-thirty sharp, even though in spring the sun is just beginning to go down.

We're all together. Eight people, two families. It's a big rectangular dark oak table, and we fit around easily. There's always enough room in the Iris family house for more. We don't even have to use fold-up chairs; there are enough dark wood ones with curvy legs for everyone and enough matching plates and knives and forks to go all around. Expensive stuff that Papa Joe left mother when he died.

Mother is dressed in a white linen mini shift. Her hair is loose on her shoulders, and she seems to shimmer against all the dark polished wood in the room.

"I always tell my girls that dinner should be a formal affair that's served punctually at the same time every day. My father always said that no matter how much insanity there was in a day some things needed to be kept constant," she says, smoothly looking at Jock, who's seated to her left. Peg is seated to Mother's right, with Otis at her side. Father is in his usual seat at the head of the table, and Streak and I sit side by side opposite Sarah and Otis.

"Room's very lovely," Peg says. I watch her as she takes in the monumental wrought-iron chandelier that hangs above the table and the matching dark oak Welsh dresser that stands behind me, with its antique willow-pattern plates displayed on the shelves. On one wall beside the Welsh dresser hangs a painting of an old Cape Dutch house in Constantia, and on the wall behind Father hangs a large oil painting of a mountain scene in the Hex River Valley. The room is as formal as the dinners we have in it. Peg and Jock, who look cleaner and neater than they did earlier in the day, look sadly shabby next to Mother's linen and Father's crisp mustard-colored shirt and silk ascot.

Lettie, her starched blue-and-white uniform crinkling loudly against her round, cushiony body, brings in the peas and rice. She keeps her head lowered when she returns from the kitchen with the roast.

Father slices the roast on its silver platter. He does it well, perfect slices, not too thick, not too thin. Mother's talking to Peg, low and private. Women's talk. Peg's hands look tired on the table next to Mother's lemon juice and Pond's-cold-cream-every-night hands.

"On the road, both born on the road," I hear Peg say. She's left Opalina in the trailer and looks naked without the snake coiled around her neck.

"Nothing like the freedom of being a wildlife photographer," Jock tells Father as he stabs a cluster of peas onto his fork. "Great way to live, but tough when money gets tight."

"Of course," Father says earnestly.

What does he know about work outdoors, I wonder. I think of him melting away every day in his warehouse of imported chocolates. Placing phone orders to confectionery stores all over the country for his assortment of fine European chocolates. His most popular are dark-covered, with bitter-tasting cherry liqueur inside. The only time I've ever seen Father outdoors at his office is when he goes to smoke a cigarette in the alley behind the warehouse, always carefully placing a white handkerchief on the packing box before he sits down, his small potbelly resting over his belt. He tells me, on one of my few visits there, that he won't allow anyone to smoke inside for fear of a fire breaking out.

While I'm imagining a hot-flamed room of melted chocolates, I catch Otis looking at me funny. His face is kind of blurred and cross-eyed looking. He eats sloppily. Red meat juice dribbling onto his faded T-shirt. I look sideways over at Streak. He's quiet like me, not saying a word, just watching everything, but he scowls across at his brother every once in a while. Mother seems even less pleased with Otis's table manners than Streak is. She drums her fingers on the edge of the table and gives Father a do-something-about-it look. Father just shrugs his narrow shoulders and clears his throat.

"What class are you in?" Peg asks Sarah in a hurried voice, as if her talking will take the attention off her messy son.

"Form three. Only two more years until I'm finished with school," Sarah says.

"Form three," Peg sighs. "Otis, Otis," she pokes him with the back of her fork. "Do you hear that? Sarah's in form three. What you'd be in, huh?"

Otis doesn't seem to hear her. He doesn't even notice when she jabs him in his side. He's begun pouring the salt and pepper shakers out in front of him in mounds, and they grow there like two mismatched mine dumps on the white tablecloth. Mother's eyes narrow, and she opens her mouth to shout for Lettie, but Sarah has already begun scooping up the salt, shoveling it with a tiny teaspoon onto her own plate.

"Thank you, Sarah," Mother says in a clipped tone, while Peg apologizes in her halting raspy voice for Otis's behavior.

I see Jock clenching his jaw and narrowing his eyes at Otis just like Mother did, only he makes his eyes into tiny narrow slits. Otis sees his father's look and backs away from the table, away from his father's stare, like it's a blow and not a hard stare his father is giving him.

"He gonna git it, git it good," Streak whispers under his breath.

I turn to look at Streak, expecting to see an angry dare-you look in his eyes. Instead I can see only the top of his head, like he pulled his neck in suddenly, the way a tortoise would retreat into its shell when it feels danger's about to come its way.

After this, Otis sits still and quiet and doesn't eat another bite. I hear Sarah sweetly telling him about our two cats, iSiCoco and inDuna, that were named by Buza, and how we just call them Coco and Duna, and also how we once had a baby donkey but that it died a few years back. Mother and Father are listening closely as Jock spins out long tales of life in the bush; how he nearly got stampeded by a herd of elephants in Kenya and how a buffalo bull almost gored him to death on a photo shoot in South West Africa.

Streak keeps humming into his shirt, "Git it, git it. He's gonna git it good," in a singsong voice and doesn't put his head up until Lettie carries in the dessert of hot baked apples and *melktert.*

After dinner Jock excuses himself and steers Otis firmly by the shoulder out of the dining room and back to the camping trailer, which has been parked in the exact spot that Mother and Father agreed upon. Jock comes back a little while later without Otis but instead brings with him a box of wildlife pictures.

"Gave that boy a stern talking-to," he says gruffly, then adds in a quieter voice, "Boy's just not used to eating at such a fancy table. Never seen silver salt and pepper shakers before."

"Worrying about the next meal, I'm afraid, Mrs. Iris, was more important than the way we ate it," Peg says apologetically to Mother.

"I'm sure he knows not to do it again," Sarah adds.

"Well, now. Let's see what's in that box, shall we?" Mother says, using her perfect mannerly way of steering unpleasant conversation in another direction.

Jock places the pictures in a stack on the dining room table, and we all crowd around while Jock takes out the first picture.

"Damn timid animal, bushbuck." Jock gently holds the corners of a glossy picture of a ram in his big hands. "Took this one in False Bay. Near impossible to get."

The rusty orange buck stares out at us, big eyes startled, wet nose glistening, ready to jump right off the smooth paper at us. There are other pictures: an African elephant in the Londolozi Game Reserve, a shot of horses and ostriches feeding in a field together in Calitzdorp in the Little Karoo, close-ups of a Burchell's zebra that he took in Maputaland. Jock handles each picture so gently, and I think how he treats his pictures as special as Peg treats Opalina. Like snakes and photographs mean more to them than anything else. The last picture that Jock shows us is of a male lion, his yellow eyes gazing straight ahead into the camera, filling the whole picture with his strong golden body.

"Magnificent," Mother murmurs, leaning closer in.

"Impressive stuff," Father says, lighting a cigarette and holding it between his teeth.

"Choose a picture each, girlies," Jock says to Sarah and me. "Go ahead. My treat. A little thank-you to your mom and dad for putting us up, but mostly for putting up with our bad ragamuffin boys."

"Oh, goody!" Sarah says excitedly.

Sarah chooses the horses and ostriches, and I take the frightened buck.

"Being a photographer must be thrilling." Sarah clutches the picture to her chest. "Just think, you get to see the wonders of the world and then capture them forever for others to enjoy."

Jock laughs appreciatively. "Couldn't have said it better myself, girlie."

"Couldn't have said it like that at all," Pegs says sharply to him in her dry-sounding voice.

Mother's lips curl in a small smile at Father, and I see them, the perfect host and hostess, shimmering, glowing brightly against the background of our new rumpled houseguests.

"Shoulda chose the lion." Streak follows me to my room after dinner.

"I liked the bushbuck more," I say, carefully taping the picture to my closet door.

"Otis once threw a stone real hard at a little buck and near killed it." Streak wipes his hands on his shorts that are already smeared with custard. "Ma says he don't know his own strength. Bet he could wallop Pa good and proper, but Pa always ties Otis up when he gives him one with the strap."

I think of smiling Jock. Warm hand in mine. This special picture he's given me. Jock with a strap hitting a tied-up boy. Pictures that won't come together in my head. The bushbuck's eyes catch mine. Run, they say. Run.

"I'm going to see Buza, our Zulu night watchman," I say hurriedly to Streak, a sudden feeling of closed-in spaces coming over me.

"I seen him as we was coming up for dinner," Streak says. "What ya want to see him for? He's just a dumb old *kaffir*."

For a second I am the lion, eyes so strong, pressing my nails into Streak's arm. "Don't ever call Buza a dumb old *kaffir* again, you hear? He's the smartest person in this whole house. Don't you dare say it again!"

"Boy, oh boy," Streak rubs his arm where I've pinched the skin. "Jeez, that's what Ma and Pa calls them. Smelly *kaffirs*.

Hell, I didn't know you was going to turn into some wildcat from just one dumb word." Streak stares hard at me, then looks away and shuffles back and forth on his feet.

Then I notice them: a circle of purple bruises around each of his ankles, like the coiled marks of a snake.

"Does your father hit you too?" I whisper.

Streak looks down at a spot between his feet and wraps his arms around himself, like a big chill suddenly came into the room, then he slowly looks up at me.

"Does he?"

"You got lotsa friends, Em'ly?" His dark eyes stare straight into mine.

"No. Not really."

"I got none." He unfolds his arms from around himself. "Take me with you to meet your old Zulu boy, an' I'll be good an' well behay-ved, I promise, Em'ly."

"You'll meet Buza another time, Streak. Not now, not today."

"Won't say no mean words to him."

"Streak, go back to the camping trailer. Tomorrow I'll take you with me to a special place."

I feel him so close beside me, feel his aloneness inside me, like it's my own.

"Tomorrow, I promise."

"No one keeps promises ever!" He says angrily, then bolts suddenly from my room.

Night Watch

By the fading light and the sudden coolness of the air, I know that Buza has already left his room in the servants' quarters at the back of the house to start his night watch. His room is small with a red polished concrete floor and an iron bed that stands on bricks to keep away the scary man—the *tokalosh*. There are tin cans with holes in them on a wooden box in his room. Magic stuff inside, he tells me. *Muthi,* to make aches and pains go away. The only decoration is a photograph of a young smiling black girl holding a baby. It's in an old frame held by a weak nail in the rough wall. I'm not supposed to be in the servants' rooms. Father's made it clear that they are off-limits, so I've only seen inside Buza's room once or twice. "Don't need you two to be interfering in the servants' lives. They know their place and you girls know yours, so stay out of their rooms. Understand?" he told Sarah and me one afternoon when he found us playing in Lettie's room that smelled of disinfectant and rose water.

As I walk down the driveway to Buza's wooden stool next to the big white pillars, I watch the light coming yellow and orange through the woods. The ribbons of colors make me think of a yellow lion chasing an orange bushbuck toward the house.

"New people staying long time, Miss Emily?" Buza asks as I sit down beside him. There are no beads for us to thread together today.

"I don't know. Father said it was just until they find another place to stay."

Buza looks out across the road toward the woods. His eyes gaze somewhere past the lake, somewhere far away.

"Miss Emily, the new lady, she have a snake, a python?" He moves his hands in a circle in front of his neck, his copper bracelets catching each other like angry bells.

"She wears it around her neck. Pretty funny, huh?" I laugh, but Buza doesn't.

"Ay, Miss Emily, that python it's a *skelm*. You know what is a *skelm*?"

"Yes, a crook, a bad man."

"*Hai*, you are right. The python, it's bad." Buza holds the top of his wooden stick, rolling his palm back and forth on its knobbled head. "This is how we Zulu know about the black soul of the python. I tell you this story because, me, I am not happy that it has come to stay with us."

I tuck my legs underneath myself and wait for Buza's voice to float down to me in the fading light.

"In the beginning, Miss Emily, people, they did not die. Death, he lived with *uNkulunkulu*, the Creator, who would not let Death go down to Earth. But Death, he begged so much with the Great One: 'Please, let me go down to Earth. Please!' So at last the Creator, he agreed.

"But the Creator, he made a special promise to First Man. He said even though he now let Death go about the earth, the people, they would not die."

"How did the Creator know that, Buza?" I lie back on the grass and look up at the sky. There are a few pale white stars already out, and I think that they are watching us as closely as I watch them.

"See, to protect them, the Creator, he put some new skins into a basket for First Man and his family, for them to wear when their bodies became too old. Then they would be young again and they would cheat Death."

Buza stands up and leans on his stick. I can tell that his legs bother him when he sits too long. After a few minutes he sits down again.

"Ay, I am getting too old, Miss Emily."

"But not old enough to have forgotten stories," I say, wanting him to carry on.

The stars are coming out fast all over the sky, and soon Mother will send Lettie to get me ready for bath and bed.

"Now, Miss Emily, the Creator, he asked the Jackal to take the basket of skins and give it to First Man. But that Jackal, *hai*, he is also no good, you know.

"On the journey, Jackal stopped in the veld. Some friends were enjoying a big meal of impala, and Jackal joined in. And he ate too much so that he fell fast asleep. While he was sleeping,

Python came and he took the basket of skins, and he slid away on his belly into the bush."

I think about the jackals I once saw in the bush, standing like beggars, waiting for the lions to finish feeding on a dead kudu. When the lions were done, the jackals ran in, barking and snapping at each other like a pack of pirate dogs.

"Well, Miss Emily, when Jackal woke up and found that the basket of skins was stolen, he ran so fast to First Man to tell him the terrible thing that has happened.

"First Man was very angry, and he cried to the Creator, 'Look what has happened to the gift of new skins!' But it was too late.

"And since that time, when people become old and their skin gets wrinkled, they must die. And that is why my people want to kill the Python when they see it.

"But Python, he's too slippery. You see, Miss Emily, he's still got those skins in the basket. So only *he* can throw off his old skin and put on a new one when his skin gets old."

Buza looks down at me. I am still on my back looking at the sky. I think how old Buza is. How wrinkled even his fingers are.

"What are you looking so long at, Miss Emily?"

"I'm looking for the Creator up there. I need to tell him to do me just one special favor—to send me only one new skin."

Buza laughs. "*Hai*, Miss Emily, a new skin for what?"

"For you, Buza, for you."

Cattery Club

In the morning, I take Streak to see my Cattery Club. From the look on his face I can see that he's half not expecting me to come down to the camping trailer to get him, but I tell him that promises shouldn't be broken and I don't break mine.

"What's a Cattery Club?" he asks as we walk around the side of the house to the back garden. He swings his arms like a free flapping bird beside me while his chameleon clings for dear life to his shoulder.

"You'll see," I tell him, feeling excited and scared about letting someone new into my special place.

The boys at school don't ever notice or talk to me. They bring Roundtree fruit pastels and Cadbury's peppermint crisps to Melody and Mindy Fairchild, the pretty, blond twins who sit behind me in class and giggle at the exact same moment at everything anyone ever says to them. Cuteness and blondness are what the boys at school seem to notice most, but Streak doesn't seem to care that I don't have either of those.

We make our way through the rows of apricot and apple

52

trees toward the farthest end of the garden. Once we get there I tell him that he needs to leave his chameleon outside.

At first he looks at me like this isn't what he's planning on doing, then he notices my hands on my hips, that I mean serious business. He grumbles about my "stupid rules" but ties the chameleon with some string to a bush and leaves it in the sun. "Won't run away. Too tame." He strokes its green scales, as if it's soft and furry, like a kitten.

Here, covered with purple bougainvillea vines, almost hidden under the poplar trees, is my Cattery Club. It was just a brown wooden playhouse until Father, in a rare moment, painted it red and white. He drew a couple of pictures of different-sized cartoon cats on it for me and wrote CATTERY CLUB across the door.

I remember how Father's face looked, blue eyes crinkled, as he dipped his brush into the red paint in the afternoon sun, the garden quiet and still. I stood watching each stroke and imagined how good it would feel to have him brush my hair. But it felt good enough anyway to watch him, so patient right then, doing something for me.

"Wow," Streak says, "special little house."

"It belongs to me. Only Sarah, Buza, Lettie, and my friend Cynthia have ever been inside."

Streak pulls at his messy dark hair and looks at me. "We be friends, right Em'ly?"

"I think so, Streak," I say quietly. "Friends means you keep promises and don't speak unkind words to each other, okay?"

"We both got dark eyes an' dark hair so'as we must be friends!" he laughs, then suddenly does a cartwheel on the grass in front of me.

"C'mon," I say, leading him inside.

Streak acts so edgy at first, like this is a palace and not a little wooden hut.

I show him my collection of cat books, the two Siamese cat statues made of glass, a marmalade cat on a poster. "I've got two real cats, Duna and Coco. Duna is expecting kittens. Have you seen them walking around outside?

"No, not see 'em yet." Streak picks up one of the statues. "Careful," I say, "they break." He quickly puts it back in its place.

"Sit down," I say.

There are two small chairs on the stone floor. Earlier in the week, I'd picked violets and put them in a glass jar on a wooden crate between the chairs. They are a bit droopy now, but you can still tell by a couple of perky petals that they had been lively violets.

Streak and I sit in the chairs and look at each other.

"Like it here," he says, playing with a hole in his shorts. "Comfy, nice."

He's the first boy I've ever let in, but I don't tell him how strangely ticklish that makes me feel inside.

"What's school like?" Streak says.

"You know."

"Never gone."

"Jeez, how do you learn?"

"Ma. In the trailer, sometimes we do lessons."

"Sometimes," I say. "Wow, are you lucky!"

"Nah, nobody to play with. Only Otis, and he's stupid." Streak points a finger at the side of his head and wiggles it in a circle.

Outside I hear Lettie singing as she hangs up the washing on the line, Xhosa songs that I don't understand but that come out of her big chest sounding full of wishing-sadness. She sings these songs every day as she hangs up clothes and sheets on the line from a washing basket that never seems to get empty.

"What's wrong with Otis?" I ask.

"I dunno, something when he was born. Nobody around to help Ma and Pa." He scratches his neck. His fingernails look pretty dirty.

"You need a bath," I say.

Streak looks upset. "I hate baths!"

"Okay," I say calmly, noticing that suddenly he looks fidgety enough to break something. "Come, let's go back to the house. Sarah's silkworms made cocoons—I'll show them to you."

As we get inside the phone starts to ring in Mother and Father's room. No one else is around, and I leave Streak with the shoebox of silkworms on the floor of my room. I run down the hallway, jump over the squeaky floorboard outside their bedroom, and grab the phone.

"Is your mother home?" a man's voice asks. I feel my breath puffy hot against the mouthpiece.

"Is your mother home?" he asks again, more slowly this

time, each word pegged separate, like the washing on the line outside. I think how much I would like to fold the words up so neatly and put them away in the back of a drawer where no one can ever find them.

"Look," he says, louder now. "Just tell me if she's home, okay?"

I run the tip of my tongue over the tiny holes of the phone to stop me from breathing too hard.

Outside the leaded bay windows a pink blossom tree *tap-taps* its branches against the glass, and I think how the man's calls to Mother keep coming just like the never-ending washing outside.

"No," I finally whisper, "she's not home." I throw the receiver onto the bedspread like it's a hot coal and run from the room, in flight now, over the floorboard that squeaks.

"Streak! Streak!" I call.

I find him sitting on the floor. He's unspun a cocoon, and what's left of it lies small and pale in his hand. He's made a hole in one side of it and has shaken the pupa out. I look at it and know it won't ever be a moth now, that I won't hear it beating its wings softly against the shoebox in the middle of the night.

Every year, when the moths are about to hatch, Sarah comes to get me. Then we wait, listening for the whirring wings, never opening the box until morning, when we cross the wet front lawn to set them free on the mulberry trees. It's the same always, just Sarah and me and the feeling that comes over me that we are doing something for the good of nature, that these little creatures get to live on an endless amount of green food in open spaces and not closed up tight in a shoebox with just a couple of air holes poked in the lid to breathe through.

I feel the pieces coming loose inside me. "Streak! Look what you've done! You can't be left alone." My voice comes out weak and unspun, like the cocoon in his guilty palm.

"Didn't mean it. Girls get so upset for nothin'!" He puts the pupa quickly in his pocket like it's a special marble I might take from him. Then he looks at me. Eyes that twist inside full of anger and shame.

"It's okay. C'mon, Streak," I say, pulling him by his arm. "Let's forget about everything that just happened. Okay?" I get a picture in my head of the receiver lying faceup on Mother's bed bleating a sick-sounding dial tone. "Let's just forget what happened and go climb the oak tree." My eyes blur and sting with tears that I won't let him see.

"Don't like high-up places," he grumbles as he follows me outside where the big oak tree stands at the front of the garden, its huge branches stretching out toward the road as if wanting to cross over to be part of the wildness of the woods.

It's too hard to explain to Streak what climbing the big oak tree feels like. Sometimes when I'm up there I pretend the tree's my whole world. Acorns to eat, branches for a bed, leaves for blankets. Safe. Away from noises of shaving cream cans being thrown in the angry bathroom before a dinner party. I can't see the steam rising from the perfumed bath. I can't hear the bathroom door slammed by Mother's fast ankle. I can't see

Father's buttons straining against his striped shirt, ringed wet under his arms from his hands that move faster than flames.

When we reach the tree, Streak looks up. "Crikey Moses!" he says. "It's too damn high."

"Suit yourself," I say, and begin to climb. I know this tree well and climb barefoot. I like the feel of bark against my skin. I know where the holes in the trunk are to put my toes, know where there's a shaky branch and where the strong ones are that I can stand on easily.

Halfway up, I hear Streak. "Wallawallawalla," he yells like some wild jungle boy. I see him through the branches as he runs toward the camping trailer and hear the door smack shut behind him.

It's quiet up here. No voices. No man's voice on the phone to hear. A voice that started the beginning of last summer and that I've heard lots of times since then. I even know his name. Dennis. Sometimes he comes to our house with his wife, Bernice, and their two daughters for lunch on Sundays. Mother met them at her tennis club at the beginning of the new season and started inviting them over. "A very likable couple, I daresay, though quite different from the usual sort you pick, Lil," Father said after their first visit. "A dentist and a home economics teacher seem much too ordinary for you!" Mother just laughed and said that Dennis had a very strong backhand and she liked that kind of challenge on the court.

Dennis is tanned like Mother, not pale and pasty-looking like Father, and he doesn't wear ascots, but open-necked shirts that show his broad, hairy chest. Sarah thinks he's a show-off, bragging about how good he is at everything. Bernice is kind-looking and always has with her a large wicker basket of half-finished tea cozies that she's in the middle of crocheting. Sometimes she brings over a new dish that she's trying out from her cooking class. Mother always makes a big fuss about the dishes and compliments Dennis on what an excellent cook his wife is. Mother herself, of course, would burn water.

Dennis never looks at me when they come over. He pretends I'm not there. That he's not the voice. I try to pretend too. Try not to hear him speak or laugh with Father. Otherwise the broken pieces feeling inside me might come back. Instead, I eat the cold chicken and potato salad on my plate and afterward take Dennis's girls outside to play and once in a while to see my Cattery Club. Only from the outside though.

I climb higher up the oak tree and think about last summer, when Dennis's phone calls to Mother began.

One of those days sticks hard inside my skin, more than all the others. It was raining like it does on lots of afternoons in summer, quick rains that come and go fast, but that make everything smell fresh and clean. Sarah and I were in my room, half naked. Sarah in one of her cool slips and me in shorts with a cotton undershirt on. We were both quietly reading, but between the sounds of pages turning was the pacing and panting sound of Mother passing the door, going back and forth down the passage from her room to mine, muttering frothy gasps of words that made no sense. Then after a good half hour, the phone suddenly rang. "About time!" Mother cried out, racing past my door to her bedroom. *Zap! Zap! Zap!* Every ring zapping my insides, like the lightning flashing through the open window.

As the rain soaked the ground outside there were no words spoken between Sarah and me. Just the *zap-zap* of the lightning and the clouds flooding the violet beds. Not long after the call, Mother, smiling and gleaming, breezed in. I looked at her over the top of my book. She had on her short white tennis dress, frilly panties showing, legs tanned.

"Girls, I'm off to play tennis," she said like she was telling us she had an invitation to have tea with the queen. Her spicy scent mixed with the wet earth smell from outside. Sarah sucked on her hair, the shut-door look in her eyes.

We both looked over at Mother and said nothing, didn't mention the rain to her. With her important plans in place it didn't exist for her right then. Didn't exist at all.

I stay up the oak tree until the sun starts to go down. I have goose bumps on my legs, but I'm not moving an inch. I see Mother's silver Buick pull in through the white pillars. Inside she strides. Outside she strides. Hands on her hips. She spots me in the tree, I'm almost to the top.

"Jesus!" she shouts, yellow dress *swish-swish*ing as she reaches the tree. "Emily, get down now!" she yells. "Do you know how high you are? What time it is?"

I blow my cheeks out. Eyes stinging. Hold my mouth full of air. Full of no answers. I throw acorns down at her. The hairspray on her hair holds one of them dead-center. She flicks it off angrily.

"Get down right now, you stubborn girl. I mean it. You're going to fall!"

I open my mouth, full of salty thoughts. "The phone's ringing," I say. "Go get it."

"No, it's not," she says impatiently. "How can it be when someone left it off the hook and I was expecting an important—" Then she pauses. "Wait," she says coldly. "I think I know what this is about." She paces around the tree a couple of times. "I need to talk to you." Her words come slow and tight. "Get down, Emily! Or I swear I'll get Buza to chop down the tree!"

"Can't"—a half-laugh, half-cry comes out—"it's too big."

"I don't need this." Mother's arms go up. "Stay there all night, then. I don't have time for this nonsense!" She trips over the fallen acorns and heads back toward the house.

Mommy, don't leave me! a voice cries in my head. *Mother!*

But she marches right through the fallen jacaranda blossoms, and I hate her for not caring. Squashes their little purple heads with the spikes of her heels.

7
Zebra Lake

A few days later the head of a murdered woman is found in Zebra Lake. Everyone at school is talking only about the crazy killing.

"Cut into pieces. Different body parts were found in separate plastic bags in lakes across the province. I can't even think about it," Sarah says, shaking the skirt of her blue school uniform up and down like it's something on her body she needs to get rid of. "The police are saying it might have been a sacrificial murder, African witchcraft." Sarah's eyes get wide. We're standing outside the school gates waiting for the bus to take us home. It's hot, too hot for spring, feels more like summer. The sun's beating onto my black lace-up school shoes, making my feet sweat in their white socks like dough rolls that have risen in the oven.

The word around school is that two boys in Sarah's class were out fishing on the lake over the weekend. At first they reeled in armloads of the thick waterweeds that grow in the water in spring, but while trying to untangle the slimy mess from their fishing lines, they discovered a woman's head in a plastic bag caught in the weeds.

"They both got sick and almost toppled the boat over." Sarah scratches her legs. There are a bunch of ruby-colored bites on them. I think of the mosquitoes that come off Zebra Lake while we sleep. Flying through the woods so quietly, through the white pillars of our driveway, passing the camping trailer, past Mother in her cream silk nightgown; past Father, slippers still on his feet, lying uncovered on top of the blankets; past me—too many cats sleeping on my bed—to Sarah they go. Asleep in her room that's cool and green, like sea foam. They hover above her pale legs, shining white in the dark, then sink themselves into her skin, suck her blood, sweet like marmalade with a spoonful of sugar in it and leave their ruby marks on her legs.

That night I dream of heads floating in plastic bags. Heads I know: Streak's chameleon, eyes bulging. Duna, her tongue swollen and purple. The last head is Mother's. She looks perfect, not even water weeds in her teeth or slime in her hair. She's smiling her tanned smile and gurgling words in giant white bubbles through the plastic bag at me. "I never told you when I was alive, I love you, Emmie, I love you." I wake hugging my pillow tightly against me.

I think about how Mother's all cut up in little pieces. A little piece for me, a little piece for Sarah and Father, a bigger piece for herself, and still the biggest piece for Dennis. There were times before Dennis when Mother had a bigger piece of herself for me. I remember the feel of her warm, silky skin against my own as I sat on her lap, maybe a dozen times or more. She would let me steer the Buick all the way home from the first bend on Winslow Lane. "Emmie," she would say, "Emmie, hop on up front, and I'll let you drive us home." Then she would pull the car over to the side of the road, and with her hands over mine and her sweet perfumed scent all around me, I would take the car, bend by bend, past the green trees as they waved us along, and I would feel right then and there that this was how I wanted us to be always. But Mother stopped it all one day last year, saying I was too big to be sitting on her lap. Not enough room to drive anymore, too squashed up, it made her feel. Not enough room for both of us behind the wheel.

Little pieces of Mother is all I get now, and the only hands that are ever over someone else's now are Sarah's over Otis's. She's taken to teaching him lots of things. How to hold a tennis racket and hit a ball up into the air. How to reel in a kite when it gets too high. How to color with different crayons in a coloring book. She's always right there behind him telling him how good he's doing and how happy it makes her feel when she sees him making progress. Sarah would make a good teacher, I think. Sarah would be great at it like she is at almost everything.

There's lots more talk about the dead lady in Zebra Lake. I hear Lettie whispering nervously on the kitchen phone about it, and at school it's the only thing on everyone's mind. No one has any clues who did it, just lots of guessing is going on. Mr. Pestano the greengrocer thinks, like most every white person in the neighborhood, that it's the work of a black person. A sacrifice of some kind done by a black witchdoctor because whites don't do such ugly crimes, according to him.

The police must be thinking the same way as Mr. Pestano because black servants are being picked up on the streets and questioned at Lakeside Police Station every day. Buza says nothing about all the police stuff going on, but I can tell he's not happy with any of it. He's moved his night-watch stool closer inside the gates of the house so he can't be spotted by a police van from the road.

"They wouldn't take you," I tell him. "You're just an old man who has to walk with a stick!"

Buza shakes his head and looks at me. "Miss Emily, the ways of the white police, there are no rules when it comes to us. They do not care if we are old or young. They see only that we are black." Buza closes his eyes and sighs, he leans back and whispers into the quiet air, "What they do not see, Miss Emily, is inside us." Buza opens his eyes and looks into my face.

"I'm sorry."

"This is not for you to feel badly about, little one. This is not your worry. I say so." Buza pats me on the shoulder with a warm hand.

"Do you think the woman found at the bottom of Zebra Lake was murdered for a black sacrifice? That's what everyone is saying."

"*Hai, Miss Emily, I cannot tell, I have not seen, I have only* heard what the people are talking. But me, I do not believe the white woman's body was used for a sacrifice. This is not our people's work."

"Tell me about your sacrifices. Tell me what they do." I lean closer to his stool, like people do when they're waiting for someone to start a spooky ghost story, half wanting and half afraid of what you might hear.

Buza laughs when he sees the look on my face.

"Ah, Miss Emily, you are a funny one." He shakes his finger at me, "You must promise me that you will stop me if you do not like what you are hearing and become afraid."

Buza takes out his snuffbox and fills his nostrils with a pinch of the dark powder before he begins.

"Sacrifice, Miss Emily, means giving something important up and hoping to get something greater back in return." Buza blows the specks of snuff off the palm of his hand. "But sometimes in life people sacrifice the wrong things. They think that what they are getting is better than what they already have." Buza laughs, seeing the puzzled look on my face. "Now I have mixed you up, let me just tell you about the old customs of sacrifice. We Zulus have two kinds of sacrifice. The first, *ukubonga,* the thanksgiving sacrifice when something good has come about. When much food has been collected, or when things are running good in the *kraal* and people have been free from sickness for a long time."

"What do you sacrifice, Buza?"

"A goat, a cow, whatever kind of animal the spirits like. Now the other kind of sacrifice is when the people of the *kraal* are dying, when things are going badly. Then we ask our ancestors, 'What have we done wrong to deserve this?' This sacrifice we call *ukuthetha*."

"How do they kill the animal?" I feel myself shiver as if the night air has passed right through me, through my colorless soul, as Buza would say.

"The thing we use to kill must be a special *assegai* that has been handed down from father to son, from father to son."

"Like your stick was passed down," I say.

"Yes, Miss Emily. But my stick, it is a spear only in spirit, only because I believe it to be one." Buza picks up his stick and gently slides his hand down its smooth wooden sides. "After the killing we give the special parts of the animal for the spirits to eat, and all the other meat the people of the *kraal* eat. We must finish before the sun goes down, but most important, we must be careful to collect all the skin and bones, and burn them so that the wizards may not take the bones and skin and make evil medicine from it."

"You don't mean *real* wizards, do you?"

"Yes, Miss Emily." Buza leans toward me and whispers, "*Umthakathi.* They are the bad ones, the enemy of the people. It is a man or a woman who uses the powers which he has learned to do bad things. Some wizards, *izinswelaboya,* we call them . . ." Buza turns his head in both directions, as if he were afraid that such a wizard was hiding in the shadows right behind him. "They use parts of the human body. Like a tongue, the lip, the eyelids, the hair, the fingernails." Buza touches each part of his body as he speaks. I grip my knees against my body and wrap my arms around them. Buza stops speaking and looks at me.

"See now, I have made you frightened, Miss Emily. This is not a good bedtime story for a little one." He clicks his tongue and shakes his head. "I am sorry you will not, I think, sleep tonight."

"Buza, please, I'm fine now. I'm just wondering still about the dead lady in Zebra Lake."

"Miss Emily." Buza holds my hands between his own. "Do not be afraid. I will never let any harm come to you. Never." Buza squeezes my fingers.

Later, I soothe myself to sleep with the sounds of his strong, gentle voice, and I dream about a stick that is mine, a stick that has the kind face of Buza carved at its top.

Picture Time

Sarah and I are having an after-two-hours-of-homework game of checkers on the front lawn when I feel warm eyes watching us. Jock. A toasty smile flashes over to us. It makes Sarah smile back and blush a little.

Jock has on the same creased khaki pants that he wore the day we met him, and his white T-shirt shows big tanned muscles where the sleeves end. Around his neck hangs a heavy-looking dark camera. I think how this is his Opalina—the thing he loves—twitching leather and metal in his strong hands.

"Fingers start itching for a good shot when I've been outta the bushveld for too long, girlies." Jock fiddles with the camera, then points it in our direction. I duck straight out of range but Sarah stands and turns toward him. Holds a pose. Dainty long leg pointed out in front of her. A curtsy for the lens.

Jock laughs, "A natural is what we have here." He moves a gadget that's attached to the camera. Zooms in closer on Sarah, who sticks her tongue out, giggles, wrinkles up her nose as Jock snap-snaps twice.

"Gotcha, sassy sheila! Tongue an' all!" Jock lowers his camera and winks at her.

Sarah's cheeks flame as red as her hair. She seems suddenly herself again with the camera not on her. It does something to her. Makes her become someone else. A sassy girl. Something she isn't.

"Let's find a nice an' pretty spot in the garden to get a few more shots, shall we, girlies?"

Sarah walks happily by his side while I lag just a few steps behind them. The game of unfinished checkers lies forgotten on the lawn.

"Camera's just a way to save a message, but in picture form." Jock squints through the lens as we walk, then suddenly spins back and aims it in my direction. Sneaky shot. I cover my eyes. I don't want him to see me. Don't want to be a message inside his black camera box.

"Aah, shy today, you are . . . picture posing not your thing, then?

"No, not mine," I say quickly.

"S'prise shots are always the best ones. Sorry, no harm meant, Em'ly. Right, then?"

I say nothing back.

"Crikey, I'm so used to shooting wild game, haven't really shot pictures of folks in years. Just don't find them as interesting as animals, see?" Then Jock adds quickly, "'Cept for you two lovely lil' sheilas, that is."

"It's okay," Sarah says in a grown-up sounding voice. "I don't find the human race all that interesting either."

"Well, lemme tell you something about the animal race. What makes 'em interesting, fact is, you can never be too sure how they're gonna react, see. People, they think animals always act predictable to their species. Folks think it's the female lion that always hunts. Not true. I've seen lotsa male lions take down an impala or two. Seen chameleons swim that weren't supposed to know how . . ."

Jock stops in front of a tree with branches that droop down, sighing with pale pink blossoms. "Stand underneath it then," he says, guiding Sarah by the elbow to the spot he wants. He positions her with one hand against its trunk and tells her to look off at some distant spot.

"Like this?" she asks, hair falling forward, her body graceful and still as her eyes gaze at a place way behind him.

Jock steps away and leans back on his heels. He uses his big hands to make a "frame" around her before reaching for his camera.

"A nyala," he says in a low, deep voice, "that's what you're like, Sarah . . . wait, one more thing." He leaps forward, shakes the tree until a flower storm of blossoms falls onto her hair, her shoulders, around her feet.

Sarah lets out a small, gleeful laugh.

"Don't move!" Jock says, quickly aiming the camera into position before he begins clicking. He speaks, all the time holding the camera on Sarah.

"A nyala's one a' the hardest an' most beautiful bucks to shoot. See, they're afraid a' us. Only way I ever shot 'em was to disguise myself as one. Found a carcass of a nyala in the bush once. Used the skin and horns an' all thrown over me to get close to one. Slender feet an' body, graceful in every way."

Sarah throws her hair to one side, leans her body closer against the tree, pale eyes under dark lashes look straight into the camera, like she's lost in his lens.

I shuffle my feet, stamp them a few times on the ground, try to get her attention, but she holds her pose, doesn't move one bit or act like she knows I'm watching. Jock's picture taking has taken her away from me.

I fiddle with my striped tie; suddenly realize that I'm still in school uniform while Sarah must have changed right after school into the pretty, cream dress that she now twirls around in before Jock's magical camera lens. I sit down on the ground a few feet away from where Jock stands, crouches, kneels as he gets the camera in the position he wants. His arms flex as he moves, veins bulge on his forearms, small sweat beads even show on his creased-up forehead. It's just the three of them that matter now. The camera, Jock, and Sarah.

"Lovely, lovely." He speaks all the time, using the right sweet, kind words that keep Sarah moving, keep her spinning and smiling in front of him.

"Know what hell would be for me?" He stops to reload the camera that's out of film. "A place far away from the smell a' raw earth, where there ain't the open clear blue sky, where I can't see the mopane tree bloom in the spring, where there's no sound of a runnin' stream and no place to watch the clouds sail by." Jock reaches in his pocket and takes out another roll of film. "Crikey, hell for me would be a four-walled house slap-bang in the middle of a big city."

"You're so lucky . . . your life is never dull," Sarah says in a dreamy voice, like she's left the city herself. She waits patiently for Jock to finish setting up the camera, straightening her shoulder straps and tucking a blossom cluster behind one ear.

"Ahh, the sight of a heavenly creature." Jock eyes her through the lens again.

"Why, thank you, sir!" She says in a sugar-sweet voice as she carefully sits herself down on the bed of blossoms beneath the tree.

Sunlight filters through its branches and bathes Sarah in soft pink light. I suck in the smell of the sweet blossoms, hold the moment like it's mine and hers. Feel her loveliness drift over in the warm breeze and take me in too. I am Sarah's pure pink beauty, dancing on a cloud, running across the veld, bathing in a stream of clear, fresh water. It's me and Sarah now in front of a camera that's full-focused on us.

Jock's words knock me back alone on the ground again.

"Know what kills beauty?" His voice catches tight in his throat. "Trophy hunters. They's what's the blight of Africa."

"Why?" Sarah asks, placing her hands in her lap, while still looking straight into the camera. But Jock lowers it, runs a hand across his damp brow. Takes a ragged cloth from his trouser pocket and wipes the lens clean.

"They kill 'em for show, a prize to pump themselves up about. Antelope horns to take home an' hang over their living room fireplaces. Impala skins to cover the entrance hall floors in their fancy homes. Bechuanaland, crikey, it used to be one a' the richest places for game in Africa, chock-full a' springbok, hartebeest, and buffalo." He places the rag in his pocket and fixes his camera gaze back on Sarah. "Almost all gone now . . ." His voice trails off.

I watch Sarah change out of the sassy style, like she's slipped out of one dress and put on another. A quiet comes over her. A sad wonder in her face.

"Poor animals," she whispers, "shot and killed for their beauty."

Jock must see the change come over her, too. Her body suddenly pulled in on itself, her arms wrapped around her knees, head hung low.

"Hold that." He directs her again as he snaps away, but slower and more planned now. "Wild game . . . we shoot 'em too, but for the moment, the memory, not for their hide or horn.

"Truth is, photographers of wild animals an' hunters, we share somethin' in common. Know what it is? See, we both have to know our animal very well, know its habitat, its favorite hidin' spots to get our shot."

Sarah looks up at him with misty eyes, soft with pain for animals she will never see or touch.

"Oh my, oh my, Sarah. Tears for the camera, what a beaut—" Jock's about to finish his sentence when a loud noise from behind startles us all. A form falling from a nearby poplar tree hits the ground with a hard thud. A bellow and a wail as Otis tries to break his fall from his hiding place.

Sarah gasps and runs toward him, a spray of blossoms bounce off her body and trail on the grass behind her while I hold back, watch Jock as he clenches his fist and yells at the heaped boy on the ground while he strides over to him.

"Spying on us you were, ya big fat fool."

"Nnnnoo . . . no, Pa. I watcha you take the piccha—"

Jock grabs him by the front of his rumpled shirt and pulls him to his feet in one hard, fast move. "From a tree? Ape hangin' in a branch, spying on me an' the young ladies while I work?"

"Me wanna watch Pa an' Sarah—"

"Pa an' Sarah, ey? Ya got some nasty thoughts cookin' in that fat heada yours?"

"Nooo, Pa—"

"Look at you, all sweaty an' worked up." Jock lets him go, shoves him backward, wipes his hand down the side of his pants like he just touched something sickening and infected.

Otis covers his head with his hands, "No hit me, Pa . . . please, no hit!" he wails.

Sarah reaches Otis's side. "He's not going to hit you. It's okay, Otis."

She holds Jock's gaze as she speaks. "No one's going to hit you."

Jock looks first at Sarah, then turns to look at me. I'm standing facing them from the same spot where I had been seated, but my legs are trapped on the ground, and the whirring in my chest makes me know that nothing inside me wants to move closer to the camera, and the crumpled boy, and the man in the khaki pants, or even to my sister's side.

Jock slowly takes the camera from his neck. "Bloomin' stupid to climb a tree when yer such a big, clumsy clod. Wanna watch me work, then y'ask permission. Understand, boy?"

"Yup, Pa; I no do again," Otis snivels, and wipes his nose on the back of his dirt-stained hand.

Jock turns to Sarah, no more toasty smile for her on his face. "Dunno if I got much here, but I'll show 'em to you when they're all done and printed. Wild game's really my thing, ya know . . ."

He turns and walks away in the direction of the camping trailer. He swings the camera loosely in his hand as if he could drop it on the ground at any second and not turn to pick it up, like a piece of gum that he's done chewing, that's lost its taste and flavor.

Only when Sarah has done calming Otis and brushing the leaves off him does she call to me. "Em, whatever are you doing so far away?"

But I don't answer her right away. Can't tell her that I know Jock will never print the pictures of her and that today will be something he will want to forget.

"Animals," I hear him say, as I stand unmoving on the ground, "fact is, you can never be too sure how they're gonna react."

As I begin to walk slowly toward Sarah and Otis, I think that it's people you can never be too sure about, even more than wild game.

A Party

Two weeks later it's Father's birthday. It seems like a good reason for them to have a party and show off our strange new houseguests to their friends. This year Mother and Father have decided it's going to be a costume party.

"The kids can help decorate when they get home from school. Hang decorations in the corners and foil stars on the ceiling," Father says at breakfast, as he spoons soft-boiled egg into his mouth. "Girls, tell Streak and Otis that they can help too."

After school, which was especially lonely because Cynthia was home with the flu, I'm counting daffodils and picking them to put in the Cattery Club. I'm at the front door of the house, on my way to the kitchen to get a vase, when I see, hanging above the front door, the head of a woman in a bloody plastic bag.

Moments later Sarah finds me, lying on the doormat, daffodils scattered across me like I'm dead.

"Em, Em," I can hear Sarah through the weeds. "It's not real, Em. It's not real."

She sits me up and goes to get one of the curvy-leg chairs from the dining room to stand on. She unhooks the plastic bag and takes it down. Otis is with her, watching everything.

"Look." Sarah holds the woman's head in front of me. "It's a mannequin head. Decoration for the party; Jock put it up this morning. He says it's meant as a joke. I think it's awful."

I start to cry and get Sarah's floral pinafore shoulder strap all wet.

"Oh, Em, I'm so sorry you're upset. It upset me too." Sarah coos softly into my hair.

Otis has the head now. He's sloshing the red water back and forth in the bag, laughing at the sound it makes.

"Give it to me, Otis," Sarah says firmly and holds out her freckled hand to him. For a moment he holds on to the bag even more tightly, but then he sees the look in her eyes and thrusts it into her hand. Otis only cares about pleasing Sarah.

He follows her day and night. From the minute she gets back from school he's there waiting to carry her book bag into the house, then he sits drooling on the floor of her room while she does her homework. He even waits outside the bathroom door, like a faithful dog would, while she takes a shower. He's become this giant mismatched shadow that's been sewn onto her, but Sarah doesn't seem to mind, or doesn't notice that his eyes are on her all the time, doesn't realize that Otis sees nothing else but her.

After some doing, Sarah gets me to calm down some. I tell her I don't know what's real and what isn't anymore, then I throw the daffodils away, even the ones that are still good and not ruined.

An hour before the party is about to begin, Mother, in a red silk Japanese robe and her hair in giant curlers, balances the phone under her chin while she stirs cheese fondue on low tables that are set out in the living room. The long cord from the kitchen phone twitches behind her. She's so busy stirring the gooey cheese that she doesn't notice me in the room.

"Can't wait. Should be fun. Mmmmm."

Bubbling laughter from Mother. More conversation.

"Don't keep me waiting like you always do. You just enjoy having the upper hand. . . ."

Then Mother spots me and waves a freshly painted nail at me, directing me out of the living room.

I shuffle off down the hallway and think about how easy it is for mother to make me go away and that maybe if I was more like the Fairchild twins at school she'd want to see me more and not make me disappear. Maybe then she might even take me with her on one of her occasional clothes shopping trips to the "Oh Yes!" boutique that's all the way in Hillbrow, in the center of Johannesburg. Mother says that if Father made the kind of money Papa Joe had made she'd shop there every day and that Papa Joe, if he was still alive, would be steaming mad that his beautiful daughter doesn't have lots of spending money for the "Oh Yes!" boutique.

I guess father calls it the "Oh No!" boutique because that's what I hear him saying to her every time she says she's going there.

Mother says that she's glad her own father is dead because he would have been sorely sad to see what kind of life his daughter is now living. Father gives her money to spend, but I guess it's never enough because she snatches the Rand bills from his hand and never even says thank you to him. She came back just the other day from a shopping trip to Hillbrow with a new mod babydoll dress and pale pink Mary Quant lipstick. "It's just the rage in London at the moment, girls," she said, tossing op-art bags with pink scrawled "Oh Yes!" across them on her bed and looking pleased as Punch with her up-to-the-fashion-minute purchases. "Sarah, want to try the lipstick on?" Mother held the silver tube out to her, but Sarah said that pale colors wouldn't suit her. I waited for mother to offer it for me to try on, but she never did.

Now, I stand in front of her vanity table and reach for the fresh-from-England magic makeup that will make her smile and say, goodness gracious, she'd never noticed it before, but her youngest daughter looks just like a dark-haired Twiggy, with her short hair and a straight up and down figure. Mother may own up-to-the-minute fashions, but her curves and shape are old fashioned now, I think to myself, and smile.

With the tube in my hand I carefully lean toward the vanity table mirror and pout my lips the way mother does when she's putting on lipstick. The little black daisy emblem on the silver tube winks at me and lets me know that Mary Quant, the nice mod lady overseas, would be happy to see how good her favorite invented color looks on me all the way down in Africa. Pinking Sheer is what it's called. While I'm closing the tube and feeling feathery soft, Mother walks in and catches me with the brand-new color on my lips. My face stains a deep shade of pink. A color no lipstick would want to be named after.

Mother laughs. Shakes her curler-covered head. "Well, who would have thought? Our little 'tomgirl' is starting to shed the tom and just be the girl." She laughs again and plucks the lipstick from my hand. She looks into my face for a second. "A little messy around the edges." She wipes the lipstick off my shaky mouth with the back of her hand, then turns to face the mirror and applies the color to her own mouth, perfectly. "That's the way it's supposed to look." She turns slowly and faces me. "Don't worry, Emily, you'll get it right sooner or later. Practice makes perfect," she says.

"Don't touch my makeup again without asking!" she yells after me, as I escape from her room.

Adult parties always sound like such fun when you hear the noise from your room. A kind of a comfort sound; laughing and glasses clinking together; more laughing, someone's made a joke; music low and smooth, sounds blending together like everything is one.

Then when you go and stand at the door and look in, it's not that way at all. Everything looks separate or in groups. Lots of empty spaces. A bowl of potato chips alone on a table, someone smoking in a corner, small circles of people with shoulders touching so no one else can squeeze in, and spilled wine where you're standing so your slippers get soggy.

Streak and Otis have been told by Peg that they're not to leave the trailer while the party's going on. Sarah stays in her room with the door closed, saying all the cigarette smoke from the room gets into her hair and clothes and stays stinking around her for weeks afterward.

I can't sleep, so I go and stand at the living room door, still wanting the comfort of adult voices, even though they sound better from far away.

The living room doors have been transformed. Purple satin is draped across the top, and silver streamers hang down from the doors like wispy curtains.

The room is dark, except for a light that makes psychedelic patterns in pink and green across the walls. It makes moldy splotches across the dancing grown-ups, the talking grown-ups, the grown-ups sitting on couches.

The sound of a woman's voice on the record player singing "Blame It on the Bossa Nova, with its magic spell," comes into me through my feet. Makes them tingle.

It's like a dream. A room of people I don't recognize right away, disguised by their costumes and the spattered light across their faces. A man in a vampire cape bites the shoulder of a lady as they dance, and laughs, a laugh I recognize as Jock's. The lady, I think, must be Peg. A woman in a witch's mask and a man dressed as a priest tango across the floor. Father, shining scalp through thin hair that can't be mistaken. He's dressed as a pirate captain, a patch over his eye, his body leaning into a rowdy round of glasses being smacked together. A woman in a shiny black dress and leopard mask touches his arm with long, red painted fingernails.

Someone notices me, half-waves at me as I stand at the door—a lady in a white dress and gold headdress. It's Mother's divorced friend, Anthea. "Isn't it bedtime, dearie?" she says through the smoke before she disappears back onto the dance floor as the crooning sounds of the latest hit, "Strangers in the Night," begins.

Smoke. There's so much smoke, clouding my eyes, filling up the spaces inside my head and making me feel thirsty, so I make my way to the kitchen for a glass of water. From the hallway I hear sounds coming from inside the pantry, muffled sounds from behind the closed door. The dull sound of cans colliding, then rolling with a thud to the floor. A catfight is my only thought as I rush to the pantry door. Duna and Coco locked up for the party in the pantry, fighting with each other, knocking cans off the shelves like ten-pins.

It is Mother's tanned legs that are spotlighted from the hallway light as the door swings open. They are between the jars of pickled onions and stewed apricots. Jars all around them and some lying knocked in a frenzy onto the floor below. Mother and Dennis. I have no breath for words in this room where the air is as thick as malt in a vat.

A fake black mustache hangs, half on, half off, across Dennis's mouth. He moans like a seal that's been beaten when he sees me, stops polishing Mother's neck with his mouth. She looks at me, her hands not large enough to cover her nakedness, her fingers searching, like she's reading Braille, for her Greek goddess sheet that lies discarded at her feet.

There are pickled onions spilled all over the floor. I step onto them, feel them burst under my feet, like eyeballs that can't see anymore. I am held stock-still in their slippery juice.

Mother throws the soiled goddess costume over her body. "Go to your room, Emily. You didn't see anything!" She covers her eyes, as if somehow by covering them it will stop me from seeing. But it is too late. I have seen, even with the smoke inside my head. I have seen it all, and I run like the bushbuck to my room and lie on my bed, smelling so strongly of the pantry that neither of the cats will come near me.

Cracked

I am cracked like Ma-we's egg. Too many pieces. But the cracks don't show for fifteen days, until I wake one night with a fever. High, like a wail in the dark, it leaps out of me.

I lie in sheets of sweat that still smell of pickled onions. The pantry has crept into my body and will not leave.

Two days go by, and still I am no better. I have become small, sharp pieces that Mother will feel in her bed. Lumpy and hard, like in *The Princess and the Pea*. I will be there, digging into her milky-white spine, so she will not sleep. Mother will not sleep, she will not sleep.

Lettie gives me soup, she spoon feeds me *mielie meal* porridge like she did when I was a baby. She rubs Vicks on my back with her sturdy hands. I am cold and chattering under blankets that won't warm me.

"*Ayzirorie!*" Lettie says when she looks into the hollowed shells of my eyes. She takes out a fresh pair of flannel pajamas and warms them on the standing heater in my room. She changes me while I am still in bed. Comfort clothes on my transparent body. Bits of honey-glue that fix me for a moment.

Then I am strong enough to be out of bed to walk to Sarah's room. She's teaching Otis to write. He's sitting at her wooden desk. I think how out of place he looks in Sarah's neat room, like a blotch-stain among her perfect things. She holds his hand and leans over him from behind and makes the letters for him. He looks up at her like she's an ice cream cone he could lick.

"Em, you're up!" Sarah says. "You were asleep when I came in earlier to check on you. Feeling any better?"

"A little, not much. I'm going back to bed."

"Otis can almost write his name. Look." Sarah sounds pleased, but I don't care to go see.

"I'm glad," I mumble. I'm already out the door when I hear her calling, "Em, Em, are you all right?"

Here's Mother. In my room. Instructions to Lettie. More soup, two spoons of cough syrup. She's called the doctor again.

When Lettie's gone for the soup, Mother stays. She runs a hand up and down the strand of pearls around her neck.

"I'm worried about you, Emily. Don't make me have to worry about you." She taps a finger against a pearl nervously. I see Peg's python around her neck instead of the pearls. The snake's blown up big, puffed up like a balloon at a birthday party. I imagine its coils tighter and tighter around Mother's neck, till her face gets purple-red and explodes. Drops of blood splattering, popping like pearls, bursting off their string onto the floor, polka-dotted across the bed where I lie.

Mother stays in the room for a while and tries to get me to

talk to her, but I'm not budging. Finally she gives up and lets out a sigh and tells me some news that she must think will make me feel better.

"Dennis and Bernice have gone to America for a dental convention," Mother says, sounding strangely unsure of herself, then leaves me in her flimsy mist of gardenias.

I sleep. An afternoon dream of Mother in a blue cashmere sweater she once wore to our school play, *Neptune's Lost Trident*. I was an oyster; Sarah, a sea horse. I wore a gray-painted cardboard shell on my front and back and a green bathing cap tight on my head. Mother hugged me afterward against the sea of her sweater, only for a moment, but I wanted to float in its blue softness forever.

I wake up to the sounds of the afternoon. The *chit-chit* of the noisy black-eyed bulbuls on the wattle tree outside my window. From the kitchen comes the tinny beat of black township music playing on the radio. The *sha-sha* of a broom sweeping leaves on the stone patio. The smell of floor polish coming strong into my room from the dining room. A cabinet door opened and the clatter of dishes being put away. Sounds that soothe me, fill me up.

Restless, in bunny slippers, I go to Mother's room to find her blue cashmere sweater. A piece of her that's soft for me to put my head on. To wrap around the cracks, like bandages on a wound.

Hidden under a pile of cardigans that smell of wet lavender, I feel sharp edges. A postcard from America. It has been disguised as a letter, secretly tucked inside an express envelope and addressed to Mrs. Lily Iris. Vicks seeps like hot flames into my chest. The radio in the kitchen is still on, but the music slinks away from my ears.

I cough up phlegm onto the postcard, infecting its foreign sand. A place called Utah, Arizona. A picture of red desert earth and a huge pillar—a totem pole—of sandstone is on the front. I turn the card over and read the scrawly black words, a spider's web that I am now trapped on.

> Lil, just arrived. Hope things have settled down on your home front with les enfants. We must talk on my return. Kids are home enjoying time with their grandma. Bernice loves America.
> See you in a few.
>
> Yours, Dennis.

Small printed words at the bottom of the card explain. Explain what? Mother and Dennis? No. Explain that "in the middle of summer, on only one day of the year, the totem pole casts a shadow of over a hundred yards across the earth. It is the longest shadow recorded in North America."

Mother and Dennis. A black shadow a hundred yards long, not just today. Forever. In Arizona, I wonder, does he think of her and smell pickled onions?

I lie on my bed and imagine myself in Arizona waiting to hear the shadow of the totem pole turn black, like the beating wings of her eyes, to cover me and snuff me out under sand and red earth.

Sunday

Day five in bed. My fever's gone and the cough too. But I like being marooned here on this island where no one can reach me.

"You're over the flu." Father stands in my room, close enough for me to smell stale cigarettes. "Come along, Emily. The fresh air will do you good." He pats the covers of my bed weakly. He has on a smart white shirt and a red silk ascot stuffed under his chin. Company must be coming over for lunch.

I stare at him, then close my eyes. Does he smell the pickled onions on her? On me? I look at him for a clue but there is none.

"Lettie!" Father shouts, turning in the direction of the door. She appears. Blue and white checked uniform and matching *doek* on her head, covering her short, curly hair under its neat tucks. I close my eyes again. Rosewater smell mixed with stale cigarettes floats through the air.

"Get Miss Emily up on her feet. She needs to get up."

"Yes, Master Bob." Lettie lowers her head, presses her hands together.

Father leaves.

"Come, Miss Emily." She sits me up, wipes my face with a warm washcloth that she brings from the bathroom, and helps me step into cotton overalls. I am the bushbuck on wobbly first legs.

"Buza, he is going to do magic before lunch for the people. It will make you to feel better." Lettie's brown soft dough arms wobble as she combs my hair. Gentle rosewater, running over me.

The veranda doors are open. Music. Frank Sinatra, Mother's favorite. His buttery voice follows me outside. The smell of T-bone steaks cooking on the *braai*. I am a wispy ghost walking, invisible in the bright sunlight.

There's Father's partner, Clive, beefy and large, sweating under his panama hat. Cigar ash perched on his big toe. His naked fat feet in sandals. His wife, Ursula, her bright yellow hair piled high on her head in a beehive, laughs with Mother as they stand under the cool shade of the plum trees. Cherry-colored drinks in their hands. Mother's lime-green sundress is pulled tight into her waist to show off its small size. Sometimes Mother even checks with a tape measure to make sure her waist stays "twenty-four inches, Emily, never more." Ursula's waist is at least thirty-five inches, according to Mother.

Jock's turning steaks for Father over the flames. Peg's stroking Opalina, like her hands need something to do. She rolls on the sides of her feet in silver sandals that look too tight. She looks uncomfortable, like she doesn't quite know where to stand or sit.

"Em, Buza's going to hypnotize the chickens before lunch." Sarah's suddenly at my side, breathy and sweet-smelling in a peach-colored dress, with Otis right behind her.

"Sit in the shade under the tree, Em. You look awful," Sarah says. I follow them to a plaid picnic blanket that's laid out under the poplar trees.

Streak appears from behind the plum tree and shuffles toward me. "Ma said you been too sick to be near." He sits down near me, then turns to give me a quick look-over. "Boy, you look kinda bad still."

"I got a disease from pickled onions," I say.

Streak looks scared. "A disease? Like something you can die from?"

"I don't think so. Don't worry, you can't catch it."

"Jeez, and Ma said you had the flu."

"That's what they all think. Parents don't know everything."

"Yeah, I know," Streak says. "They don't know nothin'." He tugs at the grass, pulls up a big clump, then tosses it down. "I met Buza all by myself when you was sick. Hope you don't mind."

"As long as you were nice to him, I don't." I say.

"He's a strange one all right. Sprinkled some hocus-pocus stuff on me. *Inteleze*, war medicine, he called it, like the chief sprinkles on his warriors, makes them strong and safe from bad stuff." Streak flexes his arms like a strong-man.

"Buza can do lots more magic, you'll see. He's going to hyp-notize the chickens," I say.

The heat's making me woozy, making me feel like a candle that's been left to melt in the sun. I can see Buza at the far end of the garden. There are four hens that live out back next to the servants' quarters. Buza is kneeling on the grass. He calls softly to them, and they come to him. He gathers them up fast by their feet, two in each hand.

Father motions to him across the lawn. "Showtime, Buza!"

Buza comes, head lowered, half-bowing to the adults who stand waiting, drinks in their white hands, in a circle on the flagstone patio.

The chickens flap and squawk, but put up no real fight. They know Buza's touch, know they are safe with him.

"Come on, let's join the others." Sarah stands and beckons to me and Streak on the picnic blanket.

Streak and I head down toward the others.

"You walking kinda funny, Emily," Streak says.

"It's because I'm still sick," I tell him. "It makes the whole world seem topsy-turvy, so I can't walk straight."

"We'll walk crooked together then," he says, zigzagging around me.

We join the others in the circle. Me next to Sarah, Streak on my other side. Buza looks at me, his eyes reaching into me, the pieces floating in the muddy liquid of his eyes.

"I do for you, Miss Emily, to make you smile," Buza says.

Lettie knows her cue and appears with a large cardboard box. Buza puts three of the chickens into it and closes the lid. With his free hand he takes a piece of white chalk from behind his ear. It leaves a faint powdery mark against his head, a small trace of warrior paint.

The chicken that Buza holds is still now, and I wonder how it must feel looking at the world upside down. The only sound is the scratching and squawking of the chickens in the box. Even Otis is standing still, his mouth open, a thread of white spit hanging loose from his bottom lip.

The heat's sealing my overalls to my body inch by inch like Saran wrap. Mother's smiling, fanning herself with a paper plate to keep cool. She's seen Buza do this so many times, she doesn't even watch anymore. Instead, she watches the faces of the guests as the chickens freeze still.

Buza puts the chicken down and holds its beak to the ground. With his other hand he draws a white chalk line from the tip of its beak straight out in front of it. The chicken's eyes are fixed on the line. It stays there. Beak to the ground. Doesn't move. Doesn't flutter even one feather.

"Bloody good!" Clive lifts his hat off and wipes his sweaty bald head with a napkin.

Buza lines up the other three chickens, one at a time, and draws chalk lines in front of them too. Beaks to the ground, the hens don't move.

Buza rubs the chalk from his hands on his faded old shorts. He looks up from his crouched position next to the chickens and smiles.

Jock laughs. "Good stuff. Your old Zulu boy's quite good. Maybe he can try to put our Otis's nose to the ground to keep him nice and well-behaved, fair dinkum! Hey, what about it, Buza?"

The adults laugh, except for Peg, who, still stroking Opalina, throws Jock a sharp look. Red hot circles appear on her leathery cheeks.

"Only joking, Peg. Hey, Buza, got any *muthi* in your pockets to bring a twinkle back into the wife's eyes?"

"No, Baas," Buza says. "I have no medicine for that." He smiles again, like he's supposed to, then stands and rubs his back.

"He's getting too old to be bending for so long," I whisper to Sarah.

"I know, Em." Sarah takes my hand and holds it to her cool cheek. "I wish you would feel better," she says softly to me.

"How long are the chickens going to stay like that?" Ursula asks, eyeing the steaks on the fire, bored already with Buza and the chickens, wanting to feed T-bone steaks to her thick waist.

"They'll stay like that forever." Mother smiles smugly as if she was the one who made it happen. Ursula looks alarmed. "Or until Buza claps his hands," Mother adds reassuringly.

"Oh, for a minute I thought we would be here all day," Ursula titters.

"Buza, old chap, clap your hands," Father commands.

"Today, my hands have no magic." Buza looks at me. "Miss Emily, she will clap her hands. She can bring the chickens back from their sleep."

"Emily looks like she's about to faint. Better give her some lemonade first." Mother gives me a concerned-mother look.

Lettie hands me some lemonade, and I take a few sips.

"Come, Miss Emily, wake the chickens up," Buza says gently.

The chickens. I can free the chickens from their cross-eyed stupor. I clap my hands. Four times. Two soft, two loud like Buza always does. The chickens sit up, squawk, surprised. They run in figure eights through the standing legs of people.

"Good job, Em!" Sarah hugs me quickly.

"Magic, Miss Emily. You make magic." Buza stands so close that I can smell his strong snuff. A ring of light from his copper bracelets shines onto the tops of my hands. Tears on the spheres. Tears that won't stop.

"Oh, Em." Sarah's peach dress is against my face as I clasp my arms about her waist.

"She's been sick. Heat must be too much for her," I hear Father tell Clive.

"She's at that emotional age," Mother tells Ursula. "Girls get like that sometimes."

"Lucky I've only got boys." Jock laughs.

I am still holding tightly on to Sarah's dress and keep my eyes shut closed and wish for more chalk-magic. Buza's chalk-magic on Mother and Father. If he held their noses to the ground and pointed them straight in my direction Mother would see that Dennis should stay in America, far away from our pantry forever. And Father would know that he shouldn't be so far away in his head all the time, and he'd see how badly I need for him to hug me just once. But mostly, I wish that they'd stay still and hypnotized long enough to feel how much I want us to be a family, all glued together with the honey wax of bees.

Later, when Clive and Ursula have gone and all that's left of the afternoon party are greasy spots of steak fat on the flagstone patio and dead-gray ash piles in the barbecue pit, Buza and I sit alone at the gates when his night-watch shift begins. I am still feeling the shakiness of sickness inside and lean against his wooden stool.

"Buza, why do grown-ups act like they know everything in the world when they don't even know what's going on right in front of them?"

"Ah, Miss Emily. This is a good question. Easy to say but hard to explain." Buza rubs his earlobes with special oil that he smears inside the huge open holes, perfect circles so large that I can see his whole neck right through them. He is preparing the spaces for new colored cork.

"Sometimes, Miss Emily, the people who make the most noise are the ones who hear the least."

Buza points an oily finger to his head then his chest. "It is the sounds in here, Miss Emily, that we must listen to. The inside voices that we cannot hear with our ears but instead feel with our hearts"

"I don't understand, Buza. What sounds are those?"

"I tell you, Miss Emily, I explain you now, but first let me put the new cork into my ear. I remember no stories when the wind is flapping through these big holes and carrying the words away with it." Buza flicks the loose skin of his earlobes and they sway back and forth like two even-swinging ropes, then he smiles down at me and gives me a wink.

"If I was little enough I could play jump rope on your ear," I tell him.

Buza laughs warmly. "*Ayziwena!* Miss Emily you say such funny things. You make me laugh like only my daughter, Matilda, makes me laugh when I see her." Buza slaps his knee and wipes his eyes, then carefully places the purple and silver corks through his gaping earlobes. When he is done, he closes his eyes and opens his palms up toward the fading sky, breathing in the cool night breeze as if he were sucking in the tale he is about to tell from the very air around us. Finally he opens his eyes and looks down at me. Eyes so soft and full of calm that I feel the shakiness leave me and something gentle glide in and take its place.

"I tell you the tale of Great Morara, Miss Emily, mighty Wolf Warrior of the Blue Mountains of Lesotho." Buza runs a hand across my eyes, willing them to close with his magic touch. "Close your eyes now, Miss Emily, and listen to the story."

I hear his voice come into me through heavy-lidded eyes, the blackness around us filled only with Buza's voice, like a soft pillow for me to rest upon.

"Mighty Morara lived at the highest point of the Maluti Mountains. He was the wisest wolf of the mountains and all that was below it. One day Bohato, a young she-cub from the pack, came to learn the great lessons that Morara had to teach. Mighty Morara sent Bohato to spend time alone in the valley, and he told her to come back when the moon was full again and tell what sounds she had heard there. When the little cub returned she told all that she had heard to the Mighty One. 'I heard the river flowing, the wind rustling, the wolf cub calling, and the birds singing,' she said. But Morara sent her back to the valley to listen more carefully."

"What more was there to hear, Buza?" I ask without my eyelids even fluttering open.

"Ah, the little she-cub was as confused as you are, Miss Emily, for she felt she had heard all that there was to hear. For a long time she sat and listened." I feel Buza's hand rest lightly on my shoulder. "For many days she heard nothing new. Then one morning as the sun was rising across the great land of Lesotho, while the shadows still covered the earth, she began to hear the very smallest new sounds." Buza pats me on the shoulder. "'These must be the new sounds,' she said, 'that the Mighty Morara wants for me to hear.'"

"What were they?" I begin to ask.

"Wait, wait, I tell you, I tell you, now." Buza holds my shoulders still with both his hands. "Bohato, she climb all the way back to the top of the Maluti peak, and there she tell the mighty Morara, 'The new, deep sounds I heard were the sound of the sun rising, the sound of the stars twinkling, and the sound of a bird's heart beating.'

"Then the mighty Wolf Warrior nodded. 'To hear the very smallest sounds inside you and in the world, that is the greatest lesson I can show you. The smallest sound, oh little Bohato, you must hear it and hold it in your heart, for it is never wrong.'

"And Bohato, Miss Emily, she never forgot the teachings of the great Morara, and she listened always to the voice inside herself. " Buza takes his hands from my shoulders and whispers to me, "Now, Miss Emily, open your eyes." He turns me gently around to face him as he crouches as best as his old body can beside me. "It is this voice that grown-ups often drown out by all the clattering they make around them," Buza says almost fiercely, looking hard into my face.

Night has come all around us, and I look up toward the house at the end of the driveway. It glows in empty white light, and I imagine Mother and Father sitting in its white darkness. Buza is silent beside me, and I hear a sound inside me, my heart beating, pulsing so very fast.

"It will be better, Miss Emily. Everything will be better one day," Buza says, and the sadness in his voice hovers in the space between us.

Even with the unusual heat this spring, there is no relief from rain. The seasons don't make new rules for badly behaved weather, and the four white chalk marks from where the chickens were hypnotized are still on the patio a week later. I am well enough, I am told by Mother, to be back in school. Seven days, after all, with the flu, seems long enough to recuperate.

School

Eighty-five of us line up in hot, cheese-smelling socks for school assembly every Friday. The principal, Mr. Coolridge, who believes everything is either black or white even though he is a gray-haired man, hasn't let a single student walk across the wooden auditorium floor in shoes in the five years since it was polished. It seems a hundred and seventy socks, sliding across its surface, collecting splinter slivers though thin wool on a weekly basis, keep up the shine just the way he likes it.

There are still whispers and talk in the auditorium about the dead lady in Zebra Lake. Body parts keep surfacing. Everything except one hand has been found. It seems everyone's lost interest in catching fish on the lake. Instead the weekend sport has become reeling in the next plastic bag of the dead lady.

I stand next to Cynthia Wright, her baby-soft blond hair thin and apologetic around her pointed face, and wait for Mr. Coolridge to give the signal for us to begin singing "All Things Bright and Beautiful."

"You missed a whole week of school. I got tired of hearing awful Emily stories at lunchtime from the 'Giggling Girls Club.'

They must have made up fifty silly reasons why you weren't at school." Cynthia rolls her blue eyes up into her head, then looks at me and adds, "You must have been quite ill."

"I'm better now," I lie.

"I'm glad." She reaches over and pulls my blue-and-red-striped school tie straight. "It's 'skew,'" she says.

While we're singing I think about her mother and mine. I wonder if things happen behind doors with Cynthia's mother and men. I picture the pantry in Cynthia's house. The spice racks that smell of parsley and paprika. The tins of biscuits that have cute pictures of puppies in baskets on them. Clear-colored bins of flour, sugar, and coffee. It is a room to store happy food in, and something inside makes me sure that there have been no strange men in their pantry.

"Your mother's so lovely. My husband thinks she could have been in movies," Mrs. Wright once said as Cynthia and I frosted a chocolate cake with her. "We could really use someone with her looks and charm on the school's fund-raising committee. It's a shame she doesn't have the time."

"Her tennis is really important to her," I told Mrs. Wright flatly.

After assembly, we search through the rows of black school shoes for our own and return in single file to our classrooms. I hear a voice whisper behind me that I've recovered from "tomboyitis." This is followed by high-pitched giggles and squeals from the Fairchild twins and the gaggle of girlie-girls behind them.

Once we are back in the classroom I force myself to concentrate on the day's lesson about how the meddling British, according to Miss Erasmus, came to the Cape Colony and forced the Afrikaans Boers to trek northwards even though they got to the Cape first. She squeaks on about how the "greedy English" rushed to take the Boers' new land again once gold and diamonds were discovered in the north and how it all led to a bloody battle called the Anglo-Boer war. I try hard to take in the dates and places and names of brave leaders on both sides, but Miss Erasmus's voice sounds dull and vague, like I'm hearing her through slimy water. I try to follow her hand as she writes words on the blackboard, but all I see is a white maze of letters that make no sense. I am a chicken looking at the world upside down, hypnotized by the chalk marks on the board.

When I get home, Streak's waiting for me on the front lawn.

"What you do in school today?" he asks.

"I don't know."

"Course you know. You was there, wasn't you?"

"Not really. Nothing made sense, like my head was all mixed up."

"It's your sickness still," Streak says. He has his chameleon with him, and he puts it on a leg of his cut-off denim shorts. We both watch as the chameleon's color changes from green to light blue.

"Wish I could change and be something else," Streak says. "Wish I could go to school like other kids do."

"Why don't you tell your mom and dad?"

"Nah." He lifts the chameleon and sets it on his arm. It starts to change to a pinkish brown color. "Wouldn't help. We move around too much."

I feel his eyes on my white school shirt, the striped blue-and-red school tie, and gray pinafore.

"Here, put the chameleon on your school tie," he says.

I take it from him and hold it still on my tie. After a few minutes the chameleon changes colors again.

"See," Streak sighs, "even a chameleon can wear a school uniform. It ain't fair." He wipes his nose on the back of his hand.

"Put your chameleon away and come inside."

From my closet I take out an old white school shirt that's frayed at the collar. I also take out a second school tie and a pair of black shorts that were always much too big and that I used for P.E. last year.

"Here, Streak. We'll make you your own special school uniform."

He takes the clothes from me. Touches them shyly, like he's almost afraid to have them in his hands. He puts his nose to them, breathes them in, and runs his fingers up and down the tie as if it's made of gold satin.

"For me?"

"For you, Streak. I don't need them."

"What'll your mother say?"

"She won't care. They're mine anyway."

Streak stands there, not sure what to do next.

"Put them on. Go ahead, they're yours now," I tell him.

There is a sweetness in the air making everything in my room spin like specks of bright sugar stirred in a glass.

Streak fumbles as he tries to button the shirt.

"Don't know how to button. Never had a shirt with buttons."

I help him with the shirt, then put the tie around his neck. We are so close that I can feel his milky breath on my face.

"When I'm all done you can look in the mirror," I say.

"Promise I can always be your friend, Emily."

I look into his dark eyes. "Yes," I say, "always." My voice sticks on the words, like they're caught at the back of my throat. I cough to unstick them. "Put the shorts on. I'll turn around," I manage to say.

I stare at the bushbuck on my cupboard while Streak changes into the shorts. I float into thoughts of Streak and me. I see us all grown up, riding in an open jeep, my cats and his chameleon on the seats behind us, surrounded by herds of bright orange bushbuck in the open grasslands that jump and flash in front of us, their silver-sparkle eyes not frightened looking like the bushbuck on my closet. The sun is going down. A ball of warm orange. It comes over us, joins us together.

"You can turn around now," Streak says.

I look at him. Except for his bare feet, he looks exactly like any of the boys in my class. Maybe a little more rumpled, like how they look after they've played a game of soccer.

Streak looks different, new to me, as if I'm meeting him for the first time. I take him by the arm, feel my heart beat through my fingers against his sleeve.

"Look," I say.

Streak stands in front of the mirror, and I step back to let him look at himself alone without another face behind him.

"Crikey Moses," he whistles through his teeth. "I look like a schoolboy, 'cept for my feet."

I get a pair of black socks from Sarah's drawer where she keeps them in matching piles.

"You don't need shoes," I tell Streak, "Mr. Coolridge doesn't let us wear them into assembly anyway."

At dinner, Jock teases Streak when he sees him in the school uniform.

"What's this we have—a little runaway schoolboy?"

"He looks real nice, real nice." Peg gently brushes Streak's hair back off his face with her fingers. It's the first time I've seen her touch anything but Opalina.

"Emily gave them clothes to me," Streak says.

Mother arches her eyebrow at me, but doesn't say a word about asking permission before I give stuff away.

"She's a sweet girl, a sweet girl," Peg says. "Later, Emily, come to the trailer. I have something for you."

There is more quiet than conversation as Peg and I walk together to the trailer so I think about Streak and his chameleon. How badly he wanted to change like it can and how easy it was for me to help him do it. I look deep into the darkness around us and wish that I could change Mother into something different. Wipe away the fashionable lipstick and tie one of Mrs. Wright's aprons around her waist. Then the phone calls might stop and she would call me Emmie. Always, and not just because she feels guilty about something. I wish hard too for something to happen so that Streak can go to school and live in one place for always. A house for Peg and Jock in our neighborhood and a permanent cage for Streak's chameleon made out of chicken wire in their new garden. Streak would go to school with me and scare the girlie-girls away with bugs and worms that he would pull out of his pocket at recess.

"Penny for your thoughts." Peg breaks the silence.

"Yes," I say shyly, but feel awkward to tell her what's on my mind.

Peg laughs a gravelly soft sound that rattles from her bony belly. She is as strange to me as the cooked garlic snail Mother once held in its shell for me to taste. Foreign and unknown. She hums a shadowy tune and seems happy that we are walking together.

When we reach the steps to the trailer, Peg takes my hand. It feels dry, like there's no liquid in her body, and I curl my fingers up in a ball so I don't have to feel the scaliness of her palm.

"It's all right," Peg says. "I know they don't feel too good, don't feel like a woman's hands should."

I nod. Ashamed that she's read my thoughts and felt me pull away from her skin.

"Weren't always like this." She holds her palms up toward the moonlight, and I look into them. Deep lines, like scorched riverbeds, run across their surface. Silver moon-water skims across the hollow spaces.

"It's on account of the fire that they got like this. Whole body feels like this, actually." She rubs her hands against each other, and I can almost see flames as her fingers crackle together.

"Fire?" I say. "You were burned?"

"Not the way you think," she laughs. "It was something I did to make a living a long time ago."

Peg opens the trailer door, and I follow her inside. The same damp pepperiness of the trailer comes at me from its walls. She lights a kerosene lamp and places it on the stove next to the copper kettle.

"Sit, please." She points for me to sit across from her at a small table next to the stove. "I've spent so many years inside this trailer, Emily. Years you wouldn't believe." She looks at me and shakes her head.

From a darkened corner of the trailer, Opalina slinks across the floor toward Peg.

"You want to know about the fire," she says, like she's read my mind again. I nod.

I look at her now, without Opalina. A scrawny throat, a spot that beats in the flickering light on her neck, her eyes darting around my face without holding still in one place.

Peg picks up the snake. It slithers up her arm, and she lets it curl around her neck. Her blond, stringy hair brushes against Opalina's coils, and the snake twitches its tail at her throat, like an angry cat.

"There was a time, after Otis was born, when things were as bad as they could be. Otis screamed, see, day and night, when he was a baby. He banged himself with his little fists on his head, like there was a pain inside so big that he wanted to tear his own head off. Jock and I would be up for days with no sleep, on account of the screaming. We sat like two hyenas in a cage, snapping at each other, we were so worn out."

Peg traces her fingers across the jagged holes in the table and runs her tongue across her thin lips a couple of times. "Jock couldn't concentrate long enough to take a single photograph, and there was no money coming in for even milk and potatoes. I took a job for a few weeks with a traveling circus. "The Fire Lady," they called me. They put this special greasy stuff all over me, then set me on fire. I would swing from a rope that was on fire too. All the lights in the circus ring were turned out, and there I was, lit up like a torch, flying through the air. Must have looked pretty amazing, like a shooting comet, don't you think?" Peg's eyes hold still on a spot behind my head as she remembers.

"Yes," I say. "But didn't it hurt a lot, the fire?"

"Some. See, the paste stuff protected me. I tried not to look down at myself and think about being on fire. But it *was* hot, very hot, and the stuff only lasted for a few seconds. On the last swing or two, as the air rushed past me I could feel the flames burning through. They doused me with a hose at the end of my act. I smelled like cooked meat for months after. Good thing was, though, that Otis quieted down around that time. I came home one night, and he was lying so quiet in his crib that I thought he was dead or something. When I picked him up he had a walloping gash on the side of his head." Peg looks away and is silent for a moment. "Jock said Otis fell clear out of his hands, he was yelling and squirming so much." Peg tugs at her loose hair and stands up suddenly.

"Knocked the demons out of him, no matter. He was a real good baby after that. Jock went back to taking pictures soon after." Peg crouches with her back to me in the corner of the trailer in search of Opalina and begins clicking her tongue softly for her snake, who had slithered suddenly away when Peg spoke of the flames and fire, as if she could feel the heat on her python skin.

I get a picture in my head of Otis's big, bloody, baby face. Drool from his mouth and eyes so flat, just like they still are.

It's quiet again, except for Opalina, who slips out of the dark corner toward Peg. She picks her up and wraps the snake like a shawl around her shoulders.

"You'd be so pretty if you'd let your hair grow, Emily. Probably look just like your mother." Peg strokes the twitching tail that rests on her chest and sighs. "You know, I'll tell you a little secret. I always wished for a daughter, but one never came. Guess it just wasn't meant to be, huh?"

"I guess not," I say. The heat from the kerosene lamp is sucking out all the coolness in the trailer, and I feel my neck grow hot and sticky.

Again, Peg seems to read my mind, and she stands to open the door. "Awful hot inside. Come sit on the steps and I'll go fetch what I said I'd give you. Jock and the boys'll be back any minute from the big house."

As I sit and wait for her on the steps I look up at the blackness and imagine Peg burning like a shooting comet across the sky holding Opalina that she uses like a rope, her rough hands holding on to the snake as they blaze their way across the universe.

The night breeze cools my neck, and I listen to the crickets singing like miniature birds under the trailer.

"Emily." Peg stands behind me. "This is for you, for being so sweet with Streak, and because I don't have no other girl in my life to give it to."

I turn toward her, and she leans down and fastens a gold chain from which hangs a little angel made of glass around my neck.

"Thank you," I say. Then, without even knowing it or planning for it to happen, we hold each other, for one long second, in the dark.

Grown-ups

They're on their way out to see a film show. Lettie hurriedly served Peg, Jock, Mother, and Father a quick parents-only dinner while we all just sat at the dining room table and watched them eat. We, "youngsters" as Father called us, would be fed dinner later by Lettie.

Born Free is what the true-life film is called. It's about a husband and wife who lived for a long time with lions in the bush. Jock tells us that he met the man and woman years ago in Kenya. He seems proud, like he had something to do with the film they're going to see.

"We sat in their tent, just feet from the lions." Jock swings his long legs over the chair, almost knocking Mother's Royal Doulton vase off the Welsh dresser. "Took months before the lions could trust them, before *they* could trust the lions. Two such damn different species, figuring out how to live together." Jock's khaki pants are clean, with no sag in the knees, and he has on a white shirt with red zigzag embroidery on the collar.

"What a fascinating life you've had. It all sounds so thrilling." Mother stands, pops a candy in her mouth off the Welsh dresser, and blows a minty kiss, aimed at no one in particular, in the direction of the table where we're still sitting. "Be good and behave, girls." she says, throwing her famous exit line at us. I wonder why she has to say "good" *and* "behave." To me they mean the same thing, but maybe to her they mean something different.

"Lettie's in charge. Dinner, homework, and bed." Father looks at Sarah and me then turns to Streak and Otis. "Back to the trailer when the girls do their homework, okay boys?" He clears his throat and musses Streak's hair on the way out the door like he's decided that's the way to act nice to a boy you don't know too well.

We move to the living room. Streak sits on the floor, leaning against the floral chintz couch, not wanting to sit on it and rumple it or anything. Sarah's in the antique yellow wood chair, legs crossed one over the other, as if this is a meeting and we're waiting for it to start. Otis stands, but not still. He's doing a balancing act along the edge of the Persian rug that has blue, gold, and red paisley designs. His arms are out like two propellers and he keeps stumbling off the edge of the rug. He opens his raw, yellow mouth and lets out a bray-laugh. It makes me want to shut him out of my head. I sit on the far side of the couch, not too close to Streak, and kick my legs back and forth.

I touch the angel necklace around my neck and think about us all; how different we are from one another, like the people in the bush with the lions. Sarah and me. Streak and Otis.

Tame and wild. Watching each other. Figuring each other out. Learning how to be friends.

Lettie appears and tells us to come and eat. She's still in her starched uniform, even though it's quite late at night. "Look. I have *pap* and meat for you all."

She puts five blue tin bowls on the low coffee table in front of us. There are no knives or forks or spoons. It's only when we are alone with her, when Mother and Father are out, that we're allowed to eat with her in her way from the servants' bowls. We eat their food—*pap* made from *mielie meal*. The sticky white porridge is mushy in your fingers as if you had put your whole hand into a fresh white bread and pulled out the stomach of the loaf.

We each take a bowl. With two fingers I mix the gravy and meat into the *pap*. "Boys' meat" is what it's called at the butcher's—servants' meat. To me it tastes better than a roast, has more flavor than Father's perfect slices. Spicy, wake-up-in-your-mouth food that could lead to some adventure.

"Yum," Streak says, dipping his whole hand into the bowl.

"My favorite food in the whole world, even though it's messy," Sarah says. She wipes her mouth and looks over at Otis, who's licking up the last drops with his tongue, the bowl tipped into his face, covering his mouth and long red chin.

When we're done, Lettie goes to the radio that's inside the corner wooden cabinet and clicks it on. She switches stations until she finds the tinny rhythm of black township music and begins dancing about the room. Round, full movements, with her hips rolling in a circle, her hands pumping the air in front of her. The music beats against the tin bowls, crosses into our living room in the white suburbs all the way from the township.

The sauce from the *pap* and gravy is on our hands and on our faces. Streak's got some on his school tie, and Sarah has a few dark red sauce strands in her hair that she doesn't know are there.

Lettie moves her hips, her apron sways to the music, swings free from the strings that tie it to her waist. "Come, Miss Sarah, Miss Emily, come dance."

Neither of us moves. Before, we always danced with Lettie. Danced and laughed and fell into bed, with the meat sauce still on our fingers. But now things feel different. There are two boys in the room.

"You dance, Sarah. I don't want to," I say.

"You're acting too shy for the boys, Miss Emily." Lettie smiles and wags her finger at me. She shakes her body, her fleshy arms wobbling hard along with the music.

Turn around, turn around my baby.
I want to see, I want to see your figure.

She sings, turning and posing for a pretend admirer. When the song comes to an end, she stops and wipes her sweaty forehead with the corner of her apron. "I go to take Buza his supper at the gates, you *tsotsies*, you must listen to what Baas Bob said. Half hour more and we must start to get ready for homework and bed."

"What we gonna do now?" Streak asks, looking down at the floor after Lettie leaves the room.

"Well, we could play checkers, jacks, or general knowledge," Sarah says.

"Don't know how to play them games." Streak frowns and looks at Sarah.

"I'll teach you, if you like." Sarah shifts in her seat, uncrosses her legs, puts her hands under the tops of her thighs.

"Teach me dance. Me dance with you, Sarah, me dance." Otis walks over to Sarah. His oversized body is like a giant curtain, blocking my view of her, but I hear her voice coming from behind him.

"Well, okay, Otis," she says slowly. "No stepping on my toes though, promise?"

Sarah walks to the radio and fiddles with the dials. Stops for a second when she hears Tommy Roe singing "Sweet Pea," then fiddles again with the dial.

I look over at Streak, half-wanting him to ask me to teach him how to dance, but he's busy looking down at the rug. Touching the blue and gold triangles in its pattern, silently moving his lips, counting shapes.

"I do that too when I'm bored or afraid," I tell him.

"I ain't 'fraid. I just don't like no dancing."

"Me too," I pretend.

Streak stops and looks up at me seriously. "Are most girls like you, Em'ly?" he asks.

"No." I laugh. "I'm one of the upside-down ones."

"Upside down's best then," he says.

I move to sit on the floor next to him. Sarah has found waltzing music and holds her hands out to Otis. She guides his hand in hers then puts his other hand on her waist. My face starts to get tight, like it's stretched out with too much air in it.

"Good, Otis. You're doing well." Sarah looks pleased, not ashamed or embarrassed at the closeness of a boy.

Lots of boys in Sarah's class seem to want to be near her and talk to her. She treats them all politely and the same like they are all so special, but not one of them is special enough for her yet.

"Streak, looka me. I do dance good, Sarah say so!" Otis grins at Streak, but Streak won't smile back.

"Gormless idiot, my brother is. Looks like a gorilla about to squash your sister to pieces," Streak snorts under his breath.

I don't answer. Don't say anything to Streak. I reach for the glass angel around my neck and hold on to it too tightly.

When the music finally ends, Otis keeps twirling Sarah around.

"Enough, it's enough. I'm getting dizzy, Otis. Stop." Sarah tries to pull away.

"More dancing, more dancing!" He holds her tight, spins her faster.

A quick flash in her eyes. I recognize the look. The eyes of the bushbuck on my closet.

"Otis, let me go!" Sarah raises her voice.

In a second, Streak is up. He throws his body onto Otis's back and bites him in the neck hard. Otis screams deep, drops to his knees, and jerks his hand to his neck. Streak's eyes are wild, his mouth red, like he just ate a plum. "Gormless idiot!" he yells.

Sarah stands still in the middle of the room. Otis is on the ground at her feet. She looks pale, dazed, like she doesn't quite know where she is.

"Sarah, are you all right?" I go to her.

"I'm fine, Em, just fine."

"Did he hurt you? He could've hurt you."

"He doesn't know his own strength. That's all. He doesn't understand."

"He scares me, Sarah, he really does," I whisper to her.

Sarah looks at me. Her blue eyes clear, like a summer sky. "He doesn't know any better."

"Sarah, you always think everything's good. You even thought the next-door dog was sweet until it bit me." I shake my head.

"What *indaba* is going on in this room?" Lettie reappears suddenly. "*This* one and *this* one are fighting here, in the house?" she points to Streak and Otis. "Up from the floor," she tells Otis. "*You*, up from the floor *now, ayzirorie!*"

Otis stands, but keeps one hand over his eyes so he doesn't have to look at anyone. "Me sorry, me sorry," he blubbers like a big baby, drool-spit running onto the Persian rug.

"It's okay," Sarah says in a flat voice. "Streak will take you back to the trailer now."

Lettie stands with her hands on her wide hips. She glares at the boys as they walk past her, Streak pushing Otis from behind.

"Night, Emily, night, Sarah," Streak mumbles, but he doesn't look at our faces.

I want to tell him that it's not his fault. That he's not to blame for Otis. That he's still my friend. But I think these things and can't get the words to be made in my mouth.

"Madam Lily and Baas Bob won't be too pleased about this." Lettie looks at Sarah and me. "These people, they are no good, no good. I think this right from the beginning. Buza, he tells me much about these people. It is better they must leave."

"Lettie, please," Sarah says. "Don't make a big fuss about this. Mother and Father don't need to know."

"They are trouble, Miss Sarah. Trouble." Lettie points her finger in the direction of the door. Her eyes fixed hard on our faces.

"I say nothing this time, but next time I will. Come, *umliliwanes,* let us get you to your rooms to do homework. Baas Bob musn't be angry with me."

Streak

Streak won't talk to me or come close to the house. He throws stones at my bedroom window then ducks down fast behind the bushes when he sees me through the glass. But I spot him, crouched down low, digging his feet deep into the dirt just the same as I would if I was trying hard to be invisible.

Once or twice I open the window wide and shout down that I can see him. But he pretends he doesn't hear, that he's just a muddy nothing on the ground.

After a couple of days I yell down, "If you had any guts you'd show your face!" This gets him hopping mad, and he jumps up and sticks out his tongue at me. When he does I look him hard and fast in the eye for a split second, but he yells back, "Lettie don't want me 'n' Otis back in the house alone ever again!"

"What happened with Otis, it's not your fault. I'm still your friend, silly!"

This time he doesn't duck down, but stands frozen-still in the mud, earthy war paint across his cheeks, brown dirt slashed across his naked chest and shorts.

"I'll talk to Lettie. Don't run away. I'm coming right down, okay, Streak? I slam the window shut and race out of the house to him, half afraid that he'll be gone forever if I don't hurry and get there fast. But when I reach him, still unmoved from his spot, the scared feeling goes away. I step, shoes and all, into the garden bed and stand close to him, like two violets planted side by side.

"Em'ly," he breathes out raspily, and I see the prickly tears on his muddy face, "is his fault, everythin's his fault!" he blurts out, his fist shaking at his sides.

I lift his hand and hold it in mine for a second. Then with the earth from his fingers glued to mine I pull him out of the muddy flower bed.

"If Otis be a normal boy, Ma fer sure wouldn'ta been 'mbarrased 'bout sendin' us to school, even for a little while at least." Streak glares angrily ahead as we sit side by side on the lawn. "She keeps us home, teaches us bits 'n' pieces holed up in that stinkin' trailer so as no one can ever see Otis at a school an' make funna him." Streak scratches his arm where the caked mud is drying. "Pa was worried 'bout Otis bein' a bully an' hurtin' someone, on account he gets wild an' mad sometimes." Streak looks over in my direction, then adds in a tough-boy voice, "Seems like Pa's strap's the only thing the gormless idiot understands real good." He smacks his head down onto his knees, "Is all his bloomin' fault, Em'ly, I swear! I'm gonna ask Buza to put a giant spell on him an' make him be gone forever."

"There's someone I wish would disappear too," I say quietly. "Wish he'd disappear—POOF!—in a cloud of smoke on the other end of the phone." I hold my arms open wide then fall back onto the soft grass and close my eyes while a voice that can't be squeezed out into thin air, no matter how tight I keep my eyes and try to push it out, echoes inside: "Is your mother home? Is your mother home?"

"Wishin' don't work, Em'ly. Wishin' never works." Streak lies down beside me on the grass.

Something inside me wants to reach out and touch his muddy fingers again.

"You promise you won't laugh if I ask you something?'

"Whatzat, Em'ly?"

I lean on my elbow to face him. "You think, maybe, I'm just a little pretty? Not like Sarah pretty but—"

"Yes," he blurts out before I even have a chance to finish speaking. "You be the prettiest most upside-down girl I ever met."

"But you've never met any other girls before!" I say, suddenly remembering.

"It don't matter, Em'ly. It don't matter one bit." He says quietly, "True is true."

Streak bends his head slowly toward mine. His lips are rabbit-fur-soft brushing against my cheek, then suddenly I feel his mouth softly touch against mine. I am liquid warm bubbles, light as a feather floating down a calm stream, a sparkling crimson jewel on a mountain high. For just one second, I am Emily the beautiful. But Streak hastily pulls away.

"Sorry," he stammers.

"Don't be." I stammer back.

The sun warms me behind my eyes, and we stay there,

Streak and I, looking up at the clear blue sky, neither of us moving, barely breathing for a long time.

"What does this mean? What does this mean, you goddamned coward!" I hear Mother's raised voice coming from behind her closed bedroom door a few days later. Sarah is out visiting a friend, and Mother and I are alone in the house after school. I can't keep myself from jumping carefully over the squeaky floorboard outside her room and pressing my ear against her closed door.

"Dennis, please! Don't do this to me, I beg you!" Mother whinnies into the phone. "Emily's just a young girl. Believe me, she's forgotten the whole thing. She's out climbing trees and playing with her little boyfriend." I feel my face burn inside, as Mother carries on: "I need you, Dennis, you have no idea—" There is a long silence, and I switch ears just to make sure that I'm still hearing properly.

Then, "I see, Dennis." I hear Mother use her slow, tight-sounding voice on him, and I feel secretly pleased. "Right. I understand," she says softly, then suddenly yells, "I understand nothing!" I hear the phone hurled hard onto the ground and Mother gasping for air, like a fish that's been thrown clear from its bowl.

I close my eyes and lean back against the door. I see Dennis, hovering above the house, floating away like a balloon. Higher and higher, close to the sun he goes, a small speck in the sky that suddenly pops, disappears. All that's left is a ragged piece of string falling back down to earth.

Mother will let me drive again I think as I tiptoe quietly back to my room. Mother will let me sit on her lap and drive.

But Mother must have found a way of keeping Dennis from escaping her completely, because now she is gone from the house even more than ever. When she is around she spends hours in front of the mirror, putting on makeup, coloring her face with pencils and little brushes that she dips into pots of blue and green and gold. False eyelashes too. Droopy little half wings that I watch her glue on above her sleek eyes, tapping them daintily with her pinkie finger.

"Mother," I say, as I stand in her bedroom doorway a few days later and watch her, her face so close to the glass that her nose almost touches the vanity table mirror. "Mother—"

"Not now, Emily. I'm busy," she says without turning around.

"Where are you going?" I ask.

"Out and about. I get bored silly staying home." She leans her body even closer to the mirror and squints at the beauty mark she's made below one eye. "There!" she says dropping the black pencil onto the vanity table, and giving herself an approving look. "Good as new." After a few more strokes of powder across her cheeks, Mother pushes herself back and stands. "What is it now, Emily?"

"I just wondered . . . Mother, could I sit on your lap like I used to and drive sometime?"

She looks at me through eyes blackened like an Egyptian princess and sighs. "Emily, you're too big now, I'm sorry. Really I am." She checks her watch and clicks her tongue. "I'm late,

I've got to go now. Tell Lettie I'll be home by dinner." She pats me on the head as she walks out the door.

I imagine her, as she skirts around me in the doorway, leaping over me, high into the sky, chasing after a balloon, reaching for its string, which she can't quite grasp, spinning farther and farther away from us, from Sarah and Father and me, even though we are all right here on the ground waiting for her. Wanting her.

Duna

She sleeps under the covers at my feet, like a hot-water bottle. Gray fuzzy belly full with kittens in their cocoons inside her.

We crown her Queen of the Cats. A small ceremony that Streak and I have in the Cattery Club. I place the glass angel necklace from Peg on Duna's head. Streak leads his chameleon that he's tied to a piece of string in a circle around her three times.

"I seen baby kittens once, come out lookin' like slug-rats," Streak tells me after the ceremony, as Duna waddles outside to lie in the sun.

"They get cute quickly," I say. "Her last litter was born in a hole out back. Come on, I'll show you."

There is a gap in the cement under the steps that's filled with brown leaves and dirt. Streak puts his hand into the hole. He lays on his stomach and peeps in, "Nothin' here, just crud and twigs," he says, disappointed, as if he's expecting to find a kitten from last year inside. "Where them kittens go?" he asks.

"Gave them away. The Greek café owner at Lakeside took two, and the other one went to a boy from school."

"We never had no ordinary pets, only Ma's snake and my chameleon and Ma's iguana what died a time back. Ma loved her iguana more'n me, for sure. Fed it the biggest, fattest bugs you ever saw. Me and Otis had to find them for her. Yelled plenty if we couldn't find none for Igqwira."

"That was the iguana's name?" I ask.

"Yeah, means witch or somethin' in Xhosa. Ma got him from a Xhosa tribe lady when we was living in the Transkei."

"How did he die?"

"Ate a bad bug, I think. Ma swears Otis and me gave him a no-good bug on purpose. Says we was jealous of Igqwira; said she'd make mincemeat out of my chameleon if anything ever happens to Opalina. Ma doesn't let us ever touch that stupid snake of hers. Like I care to, anyways. I got my own pet." Streak holds his chameleon tight to his body for a second then lets it walk up his arm.

"Were you jealous of her iguana?" I ask.

"I dunno," Streak sniffs. "Maybe, just a little." He rubs his jagged nails between the chameleon's bulging eyes.

"Why doesn't your chameleon have a name?" I ask. Streak doesn't answer right away. "Why?" I ask again.

"Things what have names always go away," Streak says in a voice that sounds like some dry twigs from the hole are stuck in his throat. "You seen all them bumper stickers on the back of our trailer, Em'ly?"

"Yes," I say.

"Zimbabwe Ruins, Port Elizabeth, Mbabane, you know, we

been to 'em all. But the places, they always go away. We never stay. I always see 'em lookin out the back window getting smaller and smaller till there's nothin' left."

That night while I'm sleeping, I feel my body suddenly shift, tilting the dream I'm having, so it hangs lopsided in my head. Movement. Mother over my bed.

"A noise, I heard a noise," I hear her say to herself or to someone outside the door who I can't see. I am awake now, but she doesn't know. She touches the blankets. Pauses.

"Oh, my God!" I hear a gasp from her lips. "Oh, Jesus!" She is out of the room. I feel for Duna at my feet, but she is between the folds of the blankets. I can hear her tongue licking furiously.

Mother comes back into the room again. I open one eye. She shines a flashlight, not on me but on her hand. It is covered in something that's brown and sticky looking.

"Emily." She shakes me with her clean hand. "Wake up. Oh, dear, you've started having your period!"

I look at her. She's still holding the flashlight spotlighted on her hand. Her eyes, fixed on the stuff on her fingers. Mother sees only her hand. She doesn't see that there's new life on my bed.

"Mother," I say and grab the flashlight from her. I shine it on my face first, pull the sheets off, and show her what I know lies inside the blankets. I hold the flashlight till it shines bright on Duna, who's licking the sticky brown stuff off her new kittens.

"Christ, Emily." Mother wipes her hand on my sheets. "You knew all the time, didn't you?" she says in that slow, special way of hers.

"If you'd have just shone the flashlight on the bed instead, you would have known, don't you see?" I cry.

"Jesus, Emily, I don't know what's the matter with you. Calm down! What a disgusting mess! God they're ugly when they're born!" She laughs, looking at the kittens. "Be a good girl, Em, and put Duna and her batch in a box," she says as she leaves the room.

I hold the flashlight under the sheets. It shines milky light on Duna and the kittens. She pulls them closer toward her with each lick. They already know to nuzzle against her, that she is warm, that she is their mother. Something races inside me. It tugs at me to lie with my head next to the wet kittens.

"Why?" I ask Sarah the next day, "Why was Mother so upset when she thought I had my period? Aren't girls supposed to get them sooner or later? Isn't twelve about right?"

"She was probably just surprised, Emily; not that you have any say in the matter when you do start. I was thirteen."

It is early afternoon, and we sit on the wooden log fence that runs for a short way around the edge of the woods. There is bark from the blue gum trees at our feet, caramel-colored wood strips that still have the rounded shape of the tree they came from. Tree skins that have fallen and left the blue gums showing pale, naked scabs.

"Tell me about it," I say.

"About what?" Sarah asks.

"Periods."

Sarah smiles, squeezes my arm, "It's not such a big deal, just some tummy cramps and blood for a few days. That's about it." She flicks her long red hair back and sighs. "Mother never talked to you about it before, did she?"

"No, she didn't," I say.

A flock of wild geese from the lake quack loudly overhead. I watch them through the trees as they land in a clear spot on the grass. I think about the rules in the goose world that I don't understand, won't ever know. Is it the goose in the front or the back who decides when they all should land, or are things decided by some special wing sign that they all know?

Sarah pats me on the knee, rubs her head against mine.

"What are you thinking about, Em?"

"About animals. There should be rules for people, like there are for animals, about how things should be done."

"You think up the most amazing things." Sarah laughs.

"Look, Sarah, Duna knew exactly what to do with her kittens when they were born. She didn't scream and carry on. She just did what she knew she should. She didn't throw a fit and yell 'Oh, lordy, oh, dear!' because they were a sticky mess."

I put my head into my hands. They smell like sour cat fur and fresh kittens because earlier I moved the whole litter in their cardboard box into the Cattery Club.

"Mother." Sarah shakes her head. "So typical of her to leave it for someone else to do her job for her. It was Lettie who explained it all to me," Sarah says. "Actually, Em, I didn't tell anyone for a few months after I got it. It made me feel . . . I don't know. . . . Then one day Lettie found me scrubbing out my panties in the bathroom sink. She explained that it wasn't a bad thing, that it was okay." Sarah pushes herself off the beam and walks to where a piece of blue gum bark lies on the ground and picks it up. "See this old bark, Emily? Well, we're kind of like trees inside. When bark gets old it falls off a tree. A period is the old stuff inside you that sheds like this blue gum bark."

I look at Sarah. The light in her hair, like a tangerine that's burst open, spilling sweet orange strands all over her pale blue dress. I think about my insides getting old before my outside, how pieces of Sarah have already gone old inside her. Sarah, my good big sister, who I'd never wish to make disappear the way Streak wishes Otis would. Sarah, who sees the whole world brighter than it really is.

"Sarah, let's not grow up," I tell her. "It doesn't seem like it's so much fun. I don't want a fat waist like Ursula or to get married and be angry at everyone all the time."

"Oh, Em, it doesn't have to be awful like that. It can be good, I really think so. I plan on meeting the most perfect boy, and we'll get married and have two children and lots of animals, and live in a charming, neat house, and I'll serve tea every afternoon at four in the living room, in pretty china cups with little red bows painted on their saucers, just wait and see!" Sarah holds the piece of bark so tight that it crumbles, flakes off in pieces onto the ground, with the sureness of her words pressing down on it.

Buza

I take the box of kittens down to him at the gates when they are three weeks old. Streak holds on to one side of the box while I hold the other. The kittens are scratching and mewing wildly, but a Sunset Naming Ceremony is important and can't be left undone.

"Swear I can pick the one I want first," Streak says.

"First one is yours, but you'd better make sure it's okay with your mom and dad," I tell him.

"Don't let Buza give my kitten a name, Em'ly."

"He'll give the other three names, but not yours, I promise."

"My own kitten, my own kitten!" Streak sings loudly all the way down the driveway.

Buza is filling his snuffbox from his pouch but looks up as we get nearer. He holds one hand out for us to stop, then puts his finger to his lips.

"Shh," he says, and closes his eyes. "Let me see now, let me listen and tell you what you have in that box of yours." He keeps his eyes closed tight and pretends to be concentrating hard. The kittens are making so much noise that even a person walking in the woods could hear them. Streak and I giggle.

"Mice," Buza says. "Little baby mice in the box, no?"

"Buza, you're teasing! It's Duna's kittens. I've brought them for you to give names."

"'Cept mine," Streak says quickly. I let go of the box, but Streak holds onto it and won't put it down until he's sure Buza agrees.

"You have given your friend a kitten?" Buza looks at me, and I nod. "And we will give it no name. That is fine, that is fine." He dusts the snuff specks off his old brown trousers and puts the snuffbox back into his pouch.

Streak and I crouch next to the box.

"Choose your kitten, Streak," I tell him.

Streak looks down into the box and touches each kitten on the head with one finger.

"This one," he says. "The one what looks like Duna."

"Good, it is settled," Buza says. "Come let me see them now, put them on my lap one at a time, so I do not need to bend."

I hand Buza a kitten. He holds its little body, looks at it in the eyes, rolls it softly between his palms onto its back, like a spongy donut.

"This one, this one is umThala. Means Milky Way, the river of white stars in the heavens. See, it is mostly black, with a white stripe across its belly. This is a good name for this kitten." He runs his hand across the line of white fur and taps the kitten on the belly before he gives it back to me.

The second kitten moves and squirms so much in his hands, as if it can feel warm hidden sparks from Buza's skin, that he names it Sina.

"*Sina* is a very lively dance in Zulu," he tells us. The third kitten he gives the name iBonsi, because of its apricot colors. "The name of the sweet wild fruit I ate when I was a boy in Zululand." Buza smacks his lips together, as if he can still taste the fruit from so many years ago.

After I return the third kitten to the box, Buza leans forward on his stool toward Streak.

"Let me look at your kitten, *umfaan*," Buza says gently to him.

Streak gets his kitten out of the box and looks nervously from me to Buza, then whispers something in the kitten's ear before handing it to Buza. It is the largest of the kittens, with a gray body and big white paws.

"Told him you was a special magic man, an' you won't do him no harm."

"Ah," Buza holds out his hands like a cradle and Streak slowly places the kitten into them. Buza strokes the kitten as it sits quietly in his palm, "You will be a cat who sees much, a *dingiswayo*, a wanderer. You will need maybe no name, but you will need *isibindi*, courage, yes, courage."

"Why courage?" I ask.

"Courage is what is needed most when a warrior does not know what lies ahead."

Streak takes the kitten from Buza like he's in a big hurry to have it back.

"Miss Emily, you tell the *umfaan*, this boy, the kitten must stay with the mother for a few more weeks, until it is weaned."

I take the kitten from Streak before he gets too attached to it and put it in the box with the others.

"Soon, Streak, just not yet, okay?" I tell him.

"Ain't fair. I always got to wait for stuff." Streak's dark eyebrows wiggle like angry caterpillars across his face.

"There are many things that will come to you, if you are patient enough to wait. Me, I believe that sometimes the waiting makes the wanting sweeter." Buza smiles and nods his head.

"What does *your* name mean anyway, Mr. Buza Magic Man?" Streak glowers at Buza and wraps his arms around his knees.

"Me"—Buza places a hand on each of his bony knees—"they called me after Buza, the captain of the young Shaka's regiment. You know Shaka, who he is? Shaka, he was king of the Zulus a long time ago. He was like no other Zulu king. My mother gave me a name of great honor, to be named after such an important warrior, the teacher of the mighty Shaka. Now the first Buza, he fought many battles. Me, I am just what we call a domestic warrior, guarding these gates—a tamed Zulu who likes to make necklaces with beads."

"Ain't no more real Zulu warriors anyways," Streak says. "Pa says they were some brute strong soldiers, an' woulda been a mighty big headache for the Afrikaners if they hadn't shot all 'em Zulus to smithereens. POW! POW! POW!" Streak points an imaginary gun in the direction of the woods.

Buza sighs and leans back, "That is so, *umfaan*, that is so." He lets out a slow quiet whistle through his teeth and looks out across the woods. I imagine him thinking of the battles he never fought, the feathered Zulu headdress he never wore, because the power of the Zulus was washed away by the Boers at the Battle of Blood River.

No one speaks, and there are no sounds, except for the mewing of the kittens that need to be returned to their mother.

The Lake

It is Sarah's idea that we all go rowing the next afternoon. There are old rowboats that can be rented from a shack at the water's edge for fifty cents an hour. The boats plod slowly around the lake like tired farm horses who've plowed the same field for too many years. In the middle of the lake is a fountain with a diamond-shaped base that has tiny windows on three sides. The idea is to row as near as you can to the fountain until you're close enough to get soaked from its smelly, saltless spray.

At night the fountain is lit up with colored lights that change every few minutes from lime green to bright pink then deep blue. I like to think that there's a dwarf-man living inside the fountain who pumps the colors at night, like icing on a cake, spurting sweet-tasting night-spray, not clear, fishy day-spray, into the lake, that no one, except the fish, gets to taste. I think how sad this makes the dwarf-man and imagine myself rowing out to the fountain one night, opening my mouth to taste the green lime, pink bubblegum, and blueberry flavored spray that he squirts up. How happy it will make the dwarf-man to see a child in summer pajamas standing shakily on a boat in the colored moonlight and drinking down his special mixes.

"The boats get locked to the dock every night. They've never allowed night boating," Father told me once when I asked about rowing to the fountain at night. But the plan to reach the fountain one night is still inside me.

I tell Streak about my idea of the dwarf-man as Sarah, Otis, Streak, and I head down through the woods to the lake.

"Jeez, Emily, ain't no way a little man, even a dwarf-man, can live inside a fountain."

"Anything's possible, Streak, that's the way I see it."

"What little man? Where little man?" Otis breathes close on my neck from behind.

"Emily's decided that there's a dwarf-man living inside the fountain at night, and I'm inclined to believe her!" Sarah walks in small light steps beside Otis, making her gingham skirt bounce away from her body with every step. Looped in the crook of her arm is a wicker basket filled with ragged pieces of old toast and dried bread for us to feed the geese.

The fifty cents in my pocket feels weighty with importance. The boat ride is twenty-five cents mine and twenty-five cents Sarah's, combined piggy-bank pocket money just waiting to be shaken out of its dark porcelain prison, to be spent on an ice cream or an outing.

We all walk over to the boat shack, and I pay the rosy-nosed boatman for the hour on the lake. He wears a dirty white T-shirt that's stretched against his flabby body like the skin of a sausage.

The boatman squints his blotchy eyes and chews on the inside of his bottom lip, like a drowsy cow chewing the cud, before picking up the money off the counter.

"Are youse all from around here?" He looks from Streak and Otis to Sarah and me.

"Yes," Sarah answers through tight lips.

"We're not. Don't live nowhere. Just stayin' with them in the house through the woods with the big white pillars," Streak points in the direction of the trees, not noticing the sharp look Sarah's giving him.

"No monkey business on the lake, you boys, *julle hoor?*" the boatman says in Afrikaans, his head rolling from Streak to Otis, who both look like they could use a comb through their hair.

"We hear," Sarah says in her most clearly pronounced English. "The oars please, mister; I mean, *meneer.*" She folds her arms across her chest and stares straight into his bloated face.

The boatman scratches under his armpit, then reaches into the barrel, where the oars are kept. "Two oars for the pretty English miss. Boat number seven." He winks at her and rolls the oars slowly, one at a time, across the wooden counter toward her, never taking his eyes off her folded arms for a minute.

Sarah snatches the oars from him before his fingers have a chance to touch her hands, spilling all the bread scraps onto the ground. Within seconds we are surrounded by geese, who hiss and snap at each other for the bread bits.

We quickly head down to the dock, where boat number seven, with peeling gray paint, is waiting for us.

"Bloody Afrikaner, makin' us beg for stupid oars. Pa says their dumb language is part slimy German language, and me and Otis don't ever got to learn it. Pa hates them Germans. Killed a whole bunch when he was in the war," Streak says.

"Bloody Afrikaner! Bloody Afrikaner!" Otis cups his hands and yells out across the lake.

"Shush up, Otis. That's not nice to yell. Come on, let's get going before the hour is up!" Sarah pulls her hair back off her neck and fans herself.

"Otis don't know how to swim too good," Streak says before we get in.

"Me do swim so good, like a shark in the water, chomp chomp." Otis makes snapping movements with his hands at Streak, then suddenly grabs Streak's head firm between his big hands and squeezes. "You tell Em'ly an' Sarah I do swim good, skunk-head!" He presses down on Streak's head harder.

"Ow, you big bully. Let go and I'll tell them!"

Otis blows hard into Streak's face, then releases him. Streak's face is beet-colored with white finger marks under his chin, where Otis held him.

"He swims like a goddamned shark. Okay!" Streak leaps into the boat so hard that it makes little waves under all the boats that are tied to the shore, and they sway higgledy-piggledy, like music notes colliding across a page.

"No fighting on the boat, Otis, or no one's going." Sarah purses her mouth.

"Me do swim good," Otis grumbles and heaves his big body into the boat, making it rock wildly back and forth.

"Sarah's a really good swimmer," I tell Streak, once we're all in. "She won second place last year in her breaststroke and butterfly races at school."

"Sarah, pretty English girl," Otis imitates the boatman and looks over at Sarah, who's seated across from him and is rowing with one oar while Streak rows with the other.

Sarah looks away, looks over the side of the boat, and for an instant I catch a glimpse of her reflection in the water, her hair like streamers around a maypole, swirling with each churning stroke.

There are only two other boats on the lake, and suddenly I feel how alone we are. I think about the hand that is still missing from the dead lady who was found at the bottom of the lake. How it might be loose and floating at this very minute below our boat, its fingers lively and free, conducting schools of fish in a circle around it.

"Think they'll ever find the missing hand?" I say.

"Sooner or later. Em, I wouldn't worry too much about it. They're pretty close to finding out who did it." Sarah pulls and dips her oar with ease.

"Bet it was that warthog-lookin' Afrikaaner boatman who done cut the lady up." Streak slaps his oar hard into the water.

"Big pieces, little pieces, lady cut in pieces!" Otis says in a singsong voice.

After about twenty minutes of rowing we're halfway across the lake, and I can begin to make out the black borders that are painted around the fountain windows. The boat's headed straight for the spray when Otis suddenly stands up.

"Pee-pee." Otis rubs his hand against his fly, as the boat lurches from side to side.

"Otis! You idiot! Sit down!" Streak yells, and butts him with the end of his oar. Otis grabs the end of the oar as it hits him in the side and pushes hard back against it, and sends Streak flying backward across the boat seat and onto the soggy floor below.

"Stop it! Stop it, you two!" Sarah spears her oar into the water to stop us from tipping over as I lean over and help Streak up. The boat tips far into the water on one side, as if the dead lady's hand is holding on to it, pulling it closer and closer into the water.

"Maniac! He's a ruddy maniac!" Streak grabs both sides of the boat to help steady it.

"Me need pee-pee!" Otis wails, clutching his trousers between his legs with both hands. Suddenly, he stops rocking. Shifts his legs together so the boat comes up even again.

One oar is lost, and the fountain looks distant and impossible to reach now.

We all watch, frozen, as a stain begins to appear like spilt water on a dark tablecloth through Otis's fingers down across his thick thighs.

"Oh, Jesus, he done pee in his pants!" Streak looks at Otis as if he's a dead dog lying in the middle of the road, covered with flies.

Otis tries to cover the wetness, cowers down until he's huddled his big mass into the corner of the boat floor.

"Me so sorry, Sarah, me done so bad. Me can't help it." He sobs so hard that the boat starts shaking again.

"Don't," Sarah says. "Don't cry, Otis, don't." She holds her hand out across the seat toward him. Otis looks up, tears streaming down his red face. He grabs her hand, holds it firm on the seat in front of him, and lays his wet cheek against the back of her palm.

Sarah's face is flushed. A small sound escapes her lips. I look at her hand that's caught under his broad cheek and watch as she turns the rest of herself away from him. Turns her body to face the water, as if her hand, like the murdered lady's, is now a separate part of her.

"Wait till Pa finds out that you done wet yourself like a bloomin' baby. He'll tan you front and back so bad with the strap, or even worse." Streak spits into both his dirty palms and rubs them together.

Otis jerks up. "No, Streaky, no! No tell Pa! No more hurting! No tell Pa!"

Streak looks over so calmly at Otis. He knows he's got him. Knows one word to Jock is all it'll take.

"Don't, Streak. Don't tell your father," I say, surprised by my own words as they come out.

"Let's just go back and forget the whole thing. We can say Otis fell into the water or something." Sarah's voice sounds tired, and her flouncy gingham skirt hangs now like wilted lettuce against her legs. She begins to row with the remaining oar, while Streak and I use our hands as oars to get us back.

"Will you tell?" I ask Streak as we get closer to shore.

"Nah. But only 'cause you don't want me to, an' also 'cause

Pa last time didn't use no strap when he found Otis, you know, touchin' hisself. He used a *knobkerrie* instead."

My hands stop in the water. The boat and lake float around me, until they come together and form a mangled picture. A picture of a stout wooden stick, carved till the top end takes the shape of a hard wooden ball and the bottom, a strong handle. A *knobkerrie*. A tribal weapon.

I walk slowly back through the woods while Sarah, Streak, and Otis go on ahead. My ears hear nothing except the squeaky voice of Miss Erasmus in history class: "Used as an execution weapon by the Zulu high command. A single fierce blow to the back of the head was all it took. I would imagine, class, that it could cause some pretty nasty bruises, even if it was used with a lighter touch on the rest of the body as a form of punishment."

There is no hurry to reach the white pillars at the end of our driveway where somewhere in the dark camping trailer I imagine a perfectly carved *knobkerrie*.

Father

I watch him through my bedroom window the next day. He angles his black Citroën around the Land Rover that's been temporarily unshackled from the camping trailer while Jock tinkers beneath its sagging body.

Father climbs out of the car, runs a hand through his thin hair, and walks with his briefcase toward the Land Rover, where Jock's legs stick out like a long-legged grasshopper's from under its front end. His face comes out from under the hood. Grins, black and greasy, at Father. Father gestures with his free hand, his mouth moving as Jock leans back against one of the Land Rover's front tires and wipes his forehead with a crumpled rag, his teeth showing. A smile or a snarl? A smile. They throw their heads back, laugh at something together.

I look at Father's briefcase and think about the boxes of sample chocolates he carries inside it. Pink satin roses imprinted on black velvet boxes. Heart-shaped chocolates wrapped in crinkly white paper that come all the way from Belgium. I remember how I once saw a boy fry ants on the pavement with the sun's rays and a magnifying glass and wonder how difficult it would be to melt the chocolates in Father's briefcase from this distance. Boil them so hot that Father could smell the chocolate bubbling, sweet and bitter in his nostrils, forcing him to stop his conversation with Jock and notice the white hole burning through his briefcase into the velvet boxes. Making his eyes travel up the sharp light to my window, where I would turn the blinding mirror away from his face. Only then, after he had to adjust his gaze, would he see me. See my face so clear that it would knock the breath right out of him. And while he smelled his fancy chocolates melting, he would know that something was not right. Father would know that something was wrong.

"Emily, run back in and get Jock a wrench from my toolbox," Father shouts out as I hurry across the lawn toward him.

I return quickly with the wrench and place it silently in his hand. "Good job, Em." Father holds onto it loosely and saunters over to Jock, crouching down to pass it to him.

A slick, oiled hand comes out from under the Land Rover. "Much obliged, mate."

My eyes watch the fingers that can hold things made of steel or wood. A hand that can fix a car or beat a boy. "Father, I need to tell you something." I bend down close toward him so the words will reach him urgently against his ear.

"In a sec. Jock's in the middle of a story," he whispers and holds his hand out over the Land Rover, like he's the Pope giving a blessing over it.

"A tough lot we were in '41. Most of us just barely twenty, or younger. Lied, I did, to get in. Sixteen, I was. But we were the bloody best. Nothin' to touch the Australian Sixth Division," Jock's voice comes out low from under the Land Rover.

Father loosens his tie and unbuttons the top of his white shirt. His briefcase lies on the strip of lawn close to the drive-way, and he stretches out on the grass beside it, leans back on his elbows, and crosses his feet at the ankles.

"Sit, Emily." He pats an empty space beside him without turning his head from the direction of the Land Rover.

I move quietly next to him, not wanting Jock to pop out yet from under the car to say a friendly hello. The sound of metal grinding scrapes like nails across my arm.

"Damn fuel pump's as stubborn as my old lady. Won't give a bloomin' inch," Jock mutters.

I fix my gaze on the spark plugs and car parts that are strewn on the driveway and imagine body pieces, smacked apart by the blows of a *knobkerrie,* strewn across the driveway instead. I hug my knees tight against my body as Jock's deep voice rolls its way out from under the Land Rover.

"Hell, where was I? Oh yeah, '41. Did we ever give them dirty Krauts a run for their money at Tobruk! Us Aussie boys bagged thirty thousand of Rommel's Jerries in one day! Blood-ied 'em an' broke 'em, we did. We was infantry, the fastest foot sloggers in Africa for sure in those days. Went in with our steel helmets and bayonets just starvin' to skewer some Kraut meat."

"Damn vicious kind of fighting, I would imagine," Father says loudly, as if he's not sure how well Jock can hear him from under the belly of the old Land Rover.

"Took their useless Jerry parts out just like this here dismembered car." Jock swings the rest of himself out from under the Land Rover. In his blackened hand is a rounded pipe with brown tubes spewing out of its sides. I shrink back farther into the ground.

"Pardon, girlie." He looks at me. "Didn't have no clue you was sittin' listenin' to all this cruddy war stuff. Crikey, the little sheila looks like she's seen a ghost or somethin'." Jock gives me a crooked grin and bounces the broken car pipe back and forth between his hands, like a hand grenade.

"She's okay. Aren't you, Emily?" Father says, shifting his hands behind his neck and glancing sideways at me. "Besides, Emily doesn't mind hearing this; she isn't one for much girl stuff. Dresses and tea parties aren't your favorite things anyway, are they, Emily?"

"No, Father, they're not," I say softly. But Father doesn't wait for my answer. He's moved on already with Jock, deeper into the war, where the noise of past gunfire drowns out my voice.

For me there is no past war to get lost in. There is only the one that seems to be happening right here in our very home. The battles between Mother and Father and the secret enemy under the car, with a hidden weapon in a drawer, a killer-soldier camouflaged as a photographer. Father doesn't see the danger, his eyes are glazed over as always, focused somewhere in the past, even when it's not his own.

"May or June, I believe it was in '41," Father says. "Half the South African army was taken prisoner by Rommel at Tobruk. You and your Sixth Division were long gone by then, I guess.

Dreadful time. I remember hearing the news on the radio in my father's mining store while I was visiting them from university in Johannesburg. I must have been almost twenty-one at the time." Father rolls over onto his side and shakes out a cigarette from his back pocket. There are grass stains on the seat of his gray slacks, and I think how long it will take Lettie to remove them; her strong hands gently massaging any trace of earth from Father's clothes on a wooden board in the laundry room out back late at night.

"Your blokes coulda' used us Aussie diggers, but we was moppin' up for MacArthur in the Philippines—nope, that was later—we was in New Guinea, I think, by then." Jock lets out a half-snort, "Bloody well near no food for our guys there in New Guinea. Wog food and bugger all of it. Desperate we was, I tell you. Can't expect to shoot straight at slit-eyed little yellow men with nothin' in your stomach." Jock reaches for the wrench again and begins tugging at the tubes till they snap like twigs torn from a bush. The sound bites into me, makes me curl my fingers inside my palms, as if it's them and not the tubes being ripped apart.

"Funny story. Happened in New Guinea, true as I'm sitting here. There we were, a bunch of Australia's pride going hungry, a good coupla days without much except Nip soup. Five of us walkin' through a jungle minefield, real easy on our feet, when suddenly, from nowhere, a pig comes squealing by us. Hell, we forgot we was on pepper-hot ground and took off like torpedoes after the rut pig." Jock cracks a piece of tubing off with his teeth and spits it onto the ground "Well, while we're

148

charging across the field, this Jewboy, Nate Stein, who's with us, keeps yellin', 'I can't eat pig! I can't eat pig!'"

"For crying out loud!" Father roars and slaps his knees so hard that the burnt end of his lit cigarette flies off and falls onto the grass beside him.

"Hell, that ain't the end of it. We was just a few yards away from the sorry beast, about to shove our bayonets right into its tasty guts"—Jock stabs the wrench into the air—"when suddenly there's this explosion. KAPOW! Right in front of us, and the pig gets blown to smithereens. Bacon bits scattered for miles. Damn animal saved our lives, and the Jewboy didn't have to watch the rest of us eat with pig fat dripping from our cheeks. Got to keep hisself pure as Moses, while Hitler made lampshades out of his Hebrew mates in Europe."

"Oh, lordy!" Father's laughing so hard that he doesn't even smell the grass starting to smolder from the cigarette ember so close to him.

"Father. Your cigarette," I blurt out. "It's burning a hole in the grass."

"Gracious, Emily." He sits up and stubs the burning ember out with the heel of his shoe. "I didn't notice. I honestly didn't notice," he says almost apologetically.

Opalina

It is feeding time, and Streak asks if maybe I'd like to watch.

"You been all gloomy last coupla' days." Streak stands in the door of my room and fiddles with a thread from his "school" shorts that have started to fray at the bottom. "Ma's got this one white mouse all ready to go in the basket. Ain't so bad, Emily. Kinda like bi'logy stuff what you learns in class."

"Where's your dad?" I ask, still not sure that I want to get off my bed.

"Gone ta see a man 'bout takin' pictures for a magazine."

"And Otis?"

"With Ma. Waitin' to watch the feedin'. C'mon, Emily. You always makin' me learn new stuff. Ma says to hurry on back. Opalina's mad as a cat, twitchin' her tail an all."

I feel pulled to follow Streak outside, half wanting, half not wanting to see Opalina eat the mouse, but his wanting to show me something new so badly is clear all over his face, so I go because that's what friends should do for each other if they are true.

Peg and Otis sit with the basket between them under the

shade of the mimosa tree at the bottom of the garden. From across the lawn it looks like a picnic's about to begin instead of a killing.

Peg wears a pair of flowered mustard shorts and a matching shirt with a blue patch over one torn pocket. Her hair, pulled tight from her face, makes her chin seem so small and sharp that if you touched its point, it would hurt. She rolls Opalina like a shiny Slinky in her hands and looks at me as we come near. Her eyes slide to the angel necklace she gave me that's around my neck.

"Glad you like it so much, Emily," she says in her raspy voice.

"Opalina's gonna slurp down that micey so fast!" Otis bounces up and down on his big seat.

"Not so fast, not so fast. It takes time." Peg snaps one stringy arm out across Otis to quiet him down, then turns to me. "Emily, you sure you wanna see this?"

"I'll watch," I say, and feel my stomach spinning out as Peg uncovers the little white mouse inside the big wicker basket.

"It ain't so bad, but if it gets too much you just turn and leave. Boys can watch anything. Girls, I know, is different." She slides Opalina into the basket. "Streaky, you and Emily sit away a little, over there." Peg points to a spot, like she's an usher directing us to the fifth row back in a movie theater.

My eyes don't leave the little mouse as it sniffs in and out of the black cloth in the bottom of the basket. I'm amazed how it doesn't even notice the huge, oily snake that's been dropped into its quiet, tiny world.

"He gonna get him good." Otis's dull eyes are stuck like a

magnet to the mouse's little pink eyes as it begins to climb, without realizing it, over the snake's scaly flesh, around the maze of her coils.

"Opalina lets 'em play for a while. She's a sweet snake," Peg says in a slippery voice.

"She likes the white ones better, hey, Ma?" Streak says.

"Seems to, boy, seems to. Look, here comes your mama, Emily." Peg straightens up, brushes down her old shorts.

The heavy scent of gardenias hits me from behind.

"You look so pretty. Going somewhere special?" Peg says quietly, looking up at Mother, who's standing right behind me.

"Lunch with a friend," Mother says quickly. "What have we here? A mouse for a snake. Is that what they eat? God, how gruesome! Emily, why in heaven's name do you want to watch this ghastly show!"

I hear Mother's stockings flare one against the other, but I don't turn around. Don't need to.

As I sit with Streak under the mimosa tree, her perfumed shadow crosses over me and I imagine the phone ringing in her bedroom. I can almost see the frosted lipstick marks where her smiling lips must have touched the mouthpiece. Can hear her voice, all satiny soft, as she makes plans to meet him today. "God, it's good to hear your voice. I miss you so. One o'clock is perfect. Can't wait."

"Emily, do you hear me? I don't think you should be watching the snake eat the mouse!" Mother taps me with a pointed fingernail on the head.

"I've seen worse things, Mother," I say, using her slow way with words, so she knows I understand. I watch the unknowing mouse as it works its way closer and closer to the snake's waiting jaws.

Mother lets out a barbed breath, snaps her purse shut, and turns on her heels. "Bye-bye, Peg, boys, Em-ily," she says giving special attention to my name.

"Have a good time," Peg shouts after her.

"Oh no!" I shriek, just as Opalina, with one striking move, swallows the mouse whole, until nothing but the tip of its pink tail can be seen between her sly, skillful jaws.

"Mousey gone sucked away!" Otis cries and copying Opalina he sticks his giant fist into his mouth, forcing his hand down his throat.

Peg whacks him hard on the back. "Stop it, you big fool. Won't we ever be able to knock some sense into that scrambled brain of yours?"

Otis takes his hand out of his mouth and stares blankly at her.

"I give up with you, Otis. Give up!" Peg's pointed chin spears the air. She reaches into the basket and strokes Opalina's scales. "Good girl. What a good girl," she coos softly to the snake.

"Watch, Emily," Streak nudges me, "watch the mouse go down inside her skin. Looks real funny, huh?"

I watch the bobbing shape inside Opalina and think about the little mouse. One minute playing in the sunlight on a mountain of round coils, then sudden darkness all around it. Where does it think it is, trapped in this long, black tunnel where there is no light, where no one can hear its squeaking growing weaker and weaker? Did no mother mouse ever teach it that a mountain of coils was dangerous and was something you ran away from? Could it have saved itself if it knew what an enemy looked like?

"I feel scared, Streak. So scared," I blurt out, standing fast, turning to run, because I can. Away from the darkness and the tunnel and the fat snake.

"Is only a mouse, is all. Is only a mouse, Emily!" Streak yells after me.

Fear

Outdoors in the open spaces, when the light is dim and Buza cannot see my face too clearly, I whisper the words against his knee and lay my cheek against his stool and tell him of the scare inside me when I imagined the mouse trapped inside the snake.

"This fear, it is not always a bad thing. A good warrior lives with fear in his heart. Even though he must be brave and strong, it is his fear that is a very important part of him." Buza tilts my head up with his bony fingers so that he can look into my face. "A fearless warrior is a dead warrior. Fear is what keeps you sharp and careful in the bush. A warrior who does not carry inside him some fear is not one to follow into battle. You understand?"

"I think so," I say, hearing suddenly the low bellow of a hippopotamus coming from the zoo across the lake.

"This fear, it must dance inside his body, but not be so great that it makes the warrior's blood freeze up so that he cannot move forward. You see?"

"Yes. It must move inside." I stand and move my body like it's a rustling tree, and wave my hands above my head, then suddenly stop, making my body stiff like stone. "But not make you freeze up." I say in a voice that sounds like the Tin Man in *The Wizard of Oz*.

"Smart Miss Emily. You are too smart." Buza chuckles as I flop back down onto the ground beside him.

"Are you afraid of anything?"

Buza does not answer right away. He jabs the tip of his stick into the ground a few times and whistles softly through his teeth before speaking.

"I am, Miss Emily, yes I am." He nods his head very slowly. "It is for my people that I fear the most. They believe that they are trapped forever, just like your little mouse inside a snake."

"But there is no way out. The little mouse died!" I cry.

Buza strokes my head with long gentle strokes. "Miss Emily, you are right—that little mouse is dead. Maybe it was not meant for him to be here any longer on the earth. Me, I must believe that perhaps the great uNkulunkulu needed him for a very special cheese party up in heaven."

I sniff and wipe my eyes with the back of my hand.

"I make a joke, but here is truth. If you believe that there is a way out, then you will find it." Buza's voice echoes in the darkness. "I fear very much for my daughter and for my grandson because my people see only the long, dark tunnel."

"What are you saying, Buza?" I look up at him, puzzled by his words.

"I am sorry, Miss Emily. I am just an old man talking without thinking; do not mind me." He pats me on the head.

"But you just said that there's always a way out if you believe. That's what you just said!"

"Yes, little one, you must always be brave and have hope. But for me, for my people, it is not always so easy."

"Doesn't anyone have hope? Not even one person, Buza?"

"There are some, a few. Yes, there are a few real warriors left, even though you cannot hear their war cry or see their feathered headdress." Buza lowers his voice, "Come, sit closer by me. Let me tell you about one little Xhosa boy who has hope." He whispers, as if there might be people listening, instead of only twinkling stars and darkness all around us.

"This warrior, he is a child of the Thembu tribe. His father gave him the name of Rolihlahla. Now, in Xhosa, Rolihlahla means 'shaking the branch of a tree.' But what it really means is someone who is not afraid to say or do what he believes, even if it gets him in trouble. He will even shake the branch of a very big tree; he is not afraid to do that.

"Now, Rolihlahla lived in a tiny village close to the waters of the Mbashe River, in a narrow, grassy valley that had many clear streams running this way and that way, and beautiful green hills all around. It was far away from Johannesburg, there in the Transkei, between the mighty Drakensberg Mountains on the one side and the beautiful Indian Ocean on the other side.

"When he was a little boy, Rolihlahla helped his mother grind the *mielies* between two stones to make the *mielie meal*. At night, he would sit around the fire with his family, and they would eat *pap* and gravy, just like you and Miss Sarah eat with Lettie sometimes. And Rolihlahla, he would listen to stories of great battles and brave Xhosa warriors. And sometimes, Miss Emily, he listened so hard to the stories, that he would forget to eat. *Hau!* Then his mother would shout, 'Hai, Rolihlahla, eat up your porridge. You must grow strong. One day you will have your own battles to fight.'

"When he grew to be an *umfaan*, a bigger boy, Rolihlahla became a herd boy, looking after sheep and cattle in the veld. While he herded the cattle with the other boys of the village, he learned how to swim and to fight with sticks with the other herd boys; and how to hit the bird from the sky with his catty— you know—slingshot. And he learned to pick berries and dig all kinds of vegetables from the ground, and to drink rich milk straight from the cow."

"Why didn't he use a cup?" I screw up my face.

"Maybe he believed it was power *muthi*, to drink the strength of a cow right from the teat. I do not know, but no matter, it is what they say about him. But, listen, Rolihlahla's father, he was one of the headmen in his tribe. Now one day there was some trouble about some lost cattle, and the magistrate who was in charge sent a message ordering Rolihlahla's father to come to him to explain about these lost cattle. But Rolihlahla's father said that he would not come. He knew this would get him in trouble, but he was not afraid to stand up against the powerful one. And his son Rolihlahla learned this from his father, to not be afraid to shake the branch of the tree."

I think of Father. About the kind of branch he might shake. I picture him under a tree that is filled with ripe, ready-to-drop imported chocolates wrapped in their colored paper. But when Father shakes the branch they all fall down on top of him. I want to tell Buza what I imagine, but he is far into his story and I think it's best not to interrupt him.

"Now in those days, Miss Emily, not too many boys and girls went to school. In fact, no one in Rolihlahla's family had ever been to school. Then one day an important man came to the village and after a few days, he says to Rolihlahla's mother, 'This *umfaan*, he is a very clever boy. You must send him to school.' So it was not to be for Rolihlahla to work on the gold mines in Johannesburg like all the other herd boys of the village. Instead, he went to school and he grew to be a very clever man.

"After many years Rolihlahla come to live here in Johannesburg, and soon he became a great leader of our people. And he fought for fairness for our people. He was never afraid to talk, even if it got him in trouble with the police."

"Is he dead now?" I ask, remembering Father once telling me that if a black man spoke up and was a problem for the police he usually landed up that way.

"No, no, he is not dead. He is in jail. The Afrikaans government, they said he is a troublemaker, and they put him in jail for life."

"Forever?" I say, hugging my knees close against my chest.

"Yes, they say for the rest of his life." Buza clicks his tongue hard against the roof of his mouth. "They take him, you know, to an island right close to Cape Town, where Baas Bob and Madam Lily take you for December holidays. Well, this Robben Island, I have heard, is not too far across the water from Cape Town. There are high walls all around, and the only way to get there is by boat." Buza smiles gently. "The government, Miss Emily, they are, I think, very afraid of this boy who shakes the branch. That is why they put him in a place like this, where there are no trees to shake and no cows to drink milk from, only stone walls and concrete floors, *hau!*"

"How horrible!" I say, wanting to make the strange, sad look on Buza's face go away. "Can anyone help him?"

"Do not worry about Rolihlahla, he is not afraid, and he will help himself. You know what Rolihlahla told the big judge there in Pretoria by the High Court before they took him away?" Buza steadies himself with his stick and slowly pulls himself up to stand as straight as his crooked back will let him before he begins. His voice is no longer a whisper, but suddenly strong and clear in the night.

"He said to the judge, 'I fought all my life for my people. I fought for fairness for my people. Not for the white man to be boss of the black man; not for the black man to be boss of the white man. But for all of us to live together in peace.'" Buza looks deep into my eyes a few moments and then he adds proudly, "And then you know what Rolihlahla said to the big judge? He said, 'This is what I believe, and this is what I hope I will do one day. And I am ready to die for what I believe.' Buza looks up into the night sky. Then he looks back down at me.

"That, Miss Emily, is the story of Rolihlahla, the boy who

has hope and who is not afraid to shake the branch of even the biggest tree." Buza sits himself carefully back down on his stool. "Inside, I am sure that Rolihlahla's fear was dancing, but it did not stop him."

"Did you ever meet him, Buza?" I ask, picturing him and Rolihlahla as great friends.

"Me? No, I do not know him. But I have seen his photo."

"Do you have his picture?"

"No. But his picture was in the newspaper just before they sent him away—on the front page. And on the top of that page it say in very big letters 'Nelson Mandela Jailed for Life.'"

"Nelson? I thought you said his name is Rolihlahla!"

"Rolihlahla is his Xhosa name; Nelson is his English name."

"How sad for Rolihlahla!"

"*Hai*, Miss Emily. But you no worry for Rolihlahla. Right now, he is stuck in the tunnel, but he will find the way out. Yes, I am sure he will find it." Buza leans back and closes his eyes, as if the telling of the tale has suddenly made him very tired.

I sit quietly at Buza's feet and think about Cape Town. My toes in the white sand, a bucket of starfish and shells in my hand. Behind me stands Table Mountain, with its huge cloud draped over it like a chiffon cloth that scarcely leaves all summer long. Across the wild, rough ocean that smells sharp and strong from all the kelp and seaweed, I imagine myself looking farther out across the foamy whitecaps where the misty sea and sky seem to meet, to a place called Robben Island, where Rolihlahla shovels gravel, covered with sweat in the hot sun, while a police guard stands over him. I remember all the times

I dug into the white beach sand, and I think how no one ever told me about the warrior across the waves until now.

"Rolihlahla," I say to Buza, "the boy who shook the branch."

"Yes, Miss Emily," Buza says softly to me in the darkness. "The boy who wasn't afraid to shake the branch."

Mother

Mother takes Sarah and me to go shopping with her at the Lakeside shops, a single row of ten stores that line one side of Randburg Avenue with the local library across the street. There's Dino's Fish and Chips; the CNA Books and Magazine store; and Greca's Café, where Greca, the bushy-eyebrowed owner, and his smiling wife will sell you homemade candies, pink-and-white coconut clusters, and creamy, velvety fudge that melts in your mouth and makes you want more before you've even finished.

There's no good reason for me to tag along except to keep Mother and Sarah company. Mother's been acting sweet and light, like angel food cake, her temper smooth and even since her "lunch with a friend" on the day Opalina swallowed the mouse. This is why I go along. To be near her when she's like this, to be sprinkled with her good-mood pixie dust that could blow away at any second. I don't even care for the moment that Dennis is the reason that there's joy in the air.

Our first stop is Mrs. Bakker's Haberdashery. They've been selling our school uniform there since Mother's school days and are the only place in Johannesburg where you can buy them. The store has a closed-in mothballs-and-linen smell that makes me want to curl up like a sleepy cat on top of one of the hundreds of bolts of colored material that fills every inch of the store. But the pointed voices of the two gray-haired ladies who run things usher us directly into the cramped far-back corner where our sacred uniforms are kept. These ladies would never allow a child to touch, let alone rest herself on, their precious fabrics.

We're here to buy Sarah new royal blue gym shorts for P.E. A note came home from her gym teacher, Mr. Radcliffe, saying that Sarah's legs have grown longer and her P.E. shorts are riding high up her thighs. It seems her legs are creating a distraction for the boys in her class. I told Sarah how Mr. Radcliffe's note made it sound as if her legs had nothing to do with her, that they were separate, growing with magical and amazing powers, like Jack's beanstalk, and could cast spells over boys without Sarah doing a thing about it.

"Magic-bean legs, that's what we'll call them from now on," I tell her as I skip alongside her down the pavement. Sarah laughs like she always does when I tell her something that she calls 'my funny way of seeing things.'

"The one who's distracted is Mr. Radcliffe himself, that toffee-nosed, muscle-bound clown. This is ridiculous," Mother scoffs as we make our way toward Mrs. Bakker's.

After Mother first read the note she said that Sarah's shorts were still perfectly respectable, but Sarah insisted that Mother take her to buy a new pair, swearing that she would never do P.E. again if Mother refused. Mother told Sarah that there would come a time when she would want to show off her legs and that having long, shapely limbs was nothing to be ashamed of, but eventually she agreed. Anyway, she said, she hadn't had an outing with her daughters alone in a while, and the three of us could stop for tea and crumpets at Lakeside Tea Room once we were done shopping.

"I'm buying an extra-large pair so that no one can even see my knees!" Sarah says, striding with her magic legs past the row of stores.

Pestano's Greengrocers is our next stop. Here, surrounded by the smell of freshly cut turnip tops and old spinach leaves, is where Mother's good mood blows away into the thin air, as pixie dust usually does.

In the aisle of butternut squashes and potatoes we run into Dennis's wife, Bernice.

"Why, hello, Bernice," Mother says, jutting her rounded chest in Bernice's direction. "Back from America? Good trip I'm sure. You certainly look well rested." Mother spins two ripe tomatoes, like tops, one in each hand, and drawls in her lah-de-dah voice.

Bernice stands with her faded brown hair and uneven complexion against a pyramid of large potatoes. She takes Mother in warmly; all her beauty stands out even more in this dreary place of boxes and crates.

"Lovely time, Lily. Dennis of course worked a lot, but the break did us good. Still, it's wonderful to be back and see old friends." Bernice looks cheerfully over at Mother, then leans forward with her lumpy vegetable bags between them and mashes Mother with her beige mouth on the cheek. Mother's green eyes open wide. Her arms fly in toward her to stop Bernice's bags from smothering the tomatoes against her cream silk blouse, then she back-steps her way out of the hug.

I look at Mother, her arms folded protectively across her chest as if to fend off another friendly attack from Bernice. She has the tomatoes still clenched tightly in her fists, and they look as if they're about to burst open, with all her hidden loathing for Bernice being squeezed into them.

Mother takes in a breath, filling herself up with fake friendliness, then breathes out in a sugar-coated voice, "Do call, Bernice, so we can have you all over for a welcome-back Sunday lunch." She flicks her thick dark hair back swiftly. "My best to Dennis. Add these to my account, Mr. Pestano," she shouts in the direction of the storage room, where I can see Mr. Pestano's squat frame bending up and down as he counts cabbage crates. Mother does a sharp about-turn and plops the tomatoes with a smooth flick of her wrists into the vegetable basket that I hold stiffly in my arms. "Girls, we need to make time. Chop-chop," she commands Sarah and me, then hurries us out onto the street.

"She really is so plain. She should do something about the color of her hair, don't you think, girls?" Mother crackles as she strides up the street toward the car, with Sarah and me following at her heels, trying hard to keep up with her fast-paced clip.

"Damn your gym teacher wanting you to blend in, Sarah.

I want my girl to be noticed! What's he trying to do? Turn you into someone who'll become a plain-Jane wife like Bernice someday!"

Mother continues her ranting and raving in the car, complaining about how Father doesn't keep her in the lifestyle that she was supposed to have, driving us all straight home in her Buick that she says should have been a Bentley. Forgetting all about the afternoon crumpets and tea she promised Sarah and me. Forgetting everything except Bernice. The wife of Dennis.

Dennis and Bentleys. The things Mother's supposed to own but doesn't.

Hide-and-Seek

Sarah and Otis against Streak and me.

"Pairs will work better," Sarah decides, since neither of the boys knows how to count to a hundred, or even close.

Streak and I race toward the servants' quarters at the far end of the garden.

"Quick," I gasp from behind the back wall. "Streak, c'mon!"

But Streak has stopped dead in his tracks in front of the open doorway to Lettie's room and won't budge. I run back and pull him by the arm. "We'll be found out if you don't come, silly!"

"I never seen no servant's room before." He leans into the room.

From the doorway the smell of Lettie's rosewater reaches us. Inside, the room is mostly empty except for Lettie's bed and a rack of clothes that hangs in one corner. A piece of red and white checkered material is strung across the small window to block out the light.

"Better'n the stinkin' trailer." Streak whistles, peering in.

"Better?" I say, thinking how small and close the room is.

"Yup. Much better. Fixed to the ground with no wheels on

168

it. Can't go anywhere, can't roll anywhere." Streak nods his head. "Servants got it better'n me. Got a home what's stuck to the ground."

"You get to travel to places I'll never see," I tell him as I pull him gently by the arm away from the open door.

We climb over tangled ivy and discarded Coke bottles to reach our hiding place, where Streak and I squeeze ourselves tight behind the back wall of the servants' quarters, not minding that there are spiderwebs and falling dust collecting in our hair.

Lettie finds us on her way to her room, before Otis and Sarah do.

"*Hai!* You filthy dirty, Miss Emily. You and your *tsotsi* boy, come out!" She puts one hand to her blue *doek,* rubs her forehead, like the messy sight of us brought on an instant headache.

"Shh, Lettie, they'll hear you. We're hiding from Sarah and Otis," I whisper.

"Miss Sarah needs to start looking for a boyfriend instead of playing hiding games. Me, I was married almost; had my first born, Constance, at seventeen." Lettie shakes her head. "Is soon suppertime, Miss Emily, you hear? Tell Miss Sarah too. Baas Bob will be home soon." She takes in the dust on my shirt and shoes one more time, then lets out a sigh. "Ay, you children," she mumbles to herself as she walks away.

Sarah and Otis find us just when I start to feel like they never will.

"If we'd been squashed behind there much longer, we woulda come out lookin' flat." Streak sneezes. "What took you two so long?"

"Sarah show me a secret place to hide." Otis's eyes glisten like a dull stone that's been wet. "Is a room outside what's fulla boxes with toys and stuff."

"Oh, Otis! You weren't supposed to tell. Now Emily knows where we're going to hide!" Sarah laughs and punches him playfully on the arm.

"The old rumpus room!" I say.

"Uh-oh. Me done bad. Me sorry, Sarah."

"It's okay. It's starting to get too dark to play anyway," Sarah says.

"I wanna see the room, too." Streak grumbles.

"It's just a storage room now," I tell Streak, "although someone named Paul once stayed in it. It's just got boxes of old toys from when Sarah and I were young. C'mon, Streak, let's go check on the kittens one more time before supper."

"Sarah done promise me I can see alla toys. I wanna see alla toys ina boxes. I not coming see no stupid kittens!" Otis says angrily.

"I didn't say you had to." I look at him, see how glazed and flat his eyes have become again, like ice on a winter pond.

"Otis." Sarah touches his arm, "Look, I promise you, I'll take you to see what's in the boxes later. After dinner and my homework's done. I said I would, okay?" She looks up at him, and I see the reflection of her face, spinning so small and perfect in the flat gray pupils of his eyes.

"Me wait after dinner for you, Sarah. Me wait."

As Streak and I walk over to the Cattery Club, I feel the coolness of night closing in and the wind start to pick up. The poplar trees bend and swing toward one another, touching their leaves in secret leaf code.

"Tree conversations," I tell Streak. "Lots of tree talk."

"What they sayin', Em'ly?'"

I cup my hand to my ear and listen to the tree sounds.

"They say they like you," I tell Streak. I take my hand down from my ear and place it on his shoulder and wish the trees had also whispered to me that one day Streak would live in a real house.

Streak's face crinkles up in a smile. "You so funny. You the funniest person I know!" He dusts off his hands on his "school uniform" that he hardly ever takes off.

As we reach the Cattery Club, he turns to me. A soft frown coming across his dark eyebrows. "I tell you a secret, Emily. I never had no other friend before you. You be my first and best friend." His words seep into me like honey. Warm glue to mend a few more cracks.

Night

Mother and Father are out late with Peg and Jock. A dinner party at Clive and Ursula's big brick house in fancy Lower Houghton. A chance for Mother to display her houseguests to the stuffy group of Father's business friends. Mother's even lent Peg a purse for the occasion. A black velvet clutch that she never uses and is meant to be carried in winter. Still, Peg seems thrilled and thanks Mother over and over again on the way out the door.

"Expect us late, very late," Mother told Lettie as she patted her upswept hairdo into place and sashayed past us in her latest purchase from the "Oh Yes!" boutique. "A Capucci original, girls. Isn't it just fabulous?" She was out the door before we had a chance to answer.

Sarah gets ready to do her homework right after Lettie feeds us a delicious cottage pie dinner. Before she leaves, Sarah leans toward Otis and whispers into his ear, making sure that Lettie, who is busy clearing away the dinner plates, doesn't notice.

Otis looks pleased and grins big and wide, nodding his head like it's on a spring even after Sarah's gone to her room.

Lettie always waits in the den until Mother and Father get home, then she stumbles in the dark to her room outside, carrying her blanket over her sleepy body. Caring for us and the house takes up most of her life.

Streak and I play a game of Snakes and Ladders before Lettie hurries the boys out the front door, pointing them sternly in the direction of the trailer. "Is bedtime for Miss Emily. She have school tomorrow, not like you *tsotsie* boys. You must go straightaway inside!" she instructs them.

Sarah's door is closed, and I think about knocking to talk to her. But I don't exactly know what about. There's something scratching inside me that needs to be shaken out, the same feeling I have when there's sand in my shoe, like I need to empty it out to feel comfortable again. I do not know what the sand is. I can't see its shape and form, but I know it's there. "Sarah, there's sand inside me," I imagine myself saying when she opens the door. And Sarah will laugh and tell me I'm the funniest person she knows. So instead I walk past her room to my own bed.

I lie staring at the nothingness of the night, listening to the spring wind blowing, picking up speed, forcing itself against the garden, against the house, until I fall asleep.

Later, the wind wakes me, blowing like a hundred fans

against my bedroom window. Rattling against the glass, like a witch's cackle. Louder and louder, the sounds hiss and laugh at me through the glass. And then through their taunting cackles a word comes hurtling out of me that jolts me up and out of bed.

Sarah. It is to Sarah I must go. The sand inside me has taken shape. The sand inside has a name.

I grope in the darkness, holding onto the wall, until I reach the familiar smooth shape of her door. The edge of her bed bumps against my legs. I feel for her in the dark. Soft pillows, gathered together, but nothing else. No sleepy breath touches me, warms my forehead as I reach across her empty sheets.

I make my way down the passageway, past Lettie's bunched-up form in the shadows of the living room floor, asleep, her thick woolen blanket covering even her head. To the kitchen I go, my mouth thick with sleep and sand, my heart thumping inside me, beating loudly like an inside war cry for Sarah, hoping that I will find her here, a late glass of milk in her hand. But here too there is no Sarah.

Through the kitchen window I see a light spilling out from under the door of the old rumpus room. The wind witches cackle even louder against the kitchen window at me. Above their screeching laughter I hear suddenly another noise, a sound of an injured animal from across Zebra Lake, only the sound is much too close!

Out the back door, I fly toward the pale glow of the rumpus room, the wind grabbing at me, whipping my pajama legs tight around my ankles. The outside room door is made of thin wood, and I throw it open without effort.

One bare lightbulb hangs from above. It lights the room like patchwork. Dark places, and light. Toys, checkered across the floor like chessmen on a board. I glimpse Sarah's old one-eyed panda bear hanging by its tangled ribbon from a toppled cardboard box.

In a lit square is Sarah. Her body pressed against the bed that has no mattress, only springs. I think how much it must hurt, the coils in her back. Her pink nightgown is lifted over her head, like a bride's veil, so lacy across her face. One small pointed nipple is free, not suffocated by Otis, who lies on top of her. He has on a gray T-shirt, but no shorts. His red, baboon bottom arches above her as he holds Sarah's face through the veil with one hand, the other around her neck, like she's a small animal needing to be tamed. She's struggling, making sounds that come out high and low, her arms and legs twitching, like a meercat that's been caught in a trap.

I stand in a dark square with no words in my head, except to stop the thumping. Stop the thing that he is doing with his raw bottom on her. I am Streak, jumping high in the night air, leaping wildly onto Otis's back, sinking my teeth into his sweaty neck, the taste of bitter rust in my mouth. With a howl, he wrenches the nightgown from Sarah, then he throws me across the room.

"Em'ly, no! No, Em'ly!" A foamy look in his eyes, as my back slams against the peeling purple paint.

Sarah breaks free. Blood runs down her legs, and I hear myself sobbing as Sarah lies gasping on the floor. She closes in on herself, like a snail into its shell, onto the ground.

I fling myself at Otis again, lunge for Sarah's nightgown,

which he grips crumpled in his hand, covering his flesh, but he slams me backward again, then he backs away.

"Me done bad! Me done bad!" he wails, and runs yelping from the room.

I crawl toward Sarah and try to cover her with my body. She bleeds red drops onto my old Russian doll and the picture books that have come apart and lie fanned out across the floor.

The witches in the wind scream at me, deafening me with their hysterical taunts. Sarah lies still beneath me, like the blood-spattered Russian doll.

"Oh, Sarah, no," I groan, not for the pain in my back, but for her. She is crying now, soft like a dove, and my hands on her long hair and my voice saying her name won't comfort her. "Sarah, please talk to me, talk to me!"

"I promised. . . . He wanted to see in the boxes. . . . My fault, my fault. . . ." Sarah moans, curling tighter inside herself, "I promised him . . . I knew it was late! Stupid, stupid me. . . ." She clutches her stomach, wraps her arms around her middle. "The old music-box, he wanted to dance. Oooh, Em, Em! Why so stupid. . . ?"

"Mommy. Daddy. Tell them, Sarah. Tell them!" I cry, holding on to her, then pulling her gently to stand and lean against my body.

"No!" Sarah lets go of me suddenly "Not anybody, Emily. You hear? Not ever! You must promise!" Her words thrown hard from her lips like a stone against my chest. She pushes away and turns from me. The springs from the bed have left red rings, like burns, on her bottom and back.

"I promise, Sarah," I sob.

Inside me, there is no more sand, only her secret that burns rings deep in my stomach.

"We need to clean up this mess. Hate mess, hate mess!" Sarah says over and over again, stuck, like the needle of a record player on a scratched album. She starts to grab at the picture book pages on the floor, then looks up. "Oh, no! Poor Panda!" She walks bent over to the cardboard box where Panda is caught midair and untangles him and holds him against herself. "I'm so sorry, Panda. I forgot all about you. Look, your stuffing's coming out. You're a mess too. Such a horrible mess!" she wails into its dusty fur.

"Sarah, please! Come with me. Please come back to the house. Bring Panda. You're so cold!" I pull her gently by her chilled arm.

"I'm naked. Oh, God, I'm naked!" Sarah cries as we go back to the house, with Panda still clutched to her body. "Stupid and naked, stupid and naked!" she whimpers over and over again.

We pass Lettie, still covered with her blanket, asleep on the living room floor. I stop, but Sarah pulls me, "Nobody, Emily! Nobody! You promised!"

In her bed we lie, curled like two spoons against each other. I comb her hair with my hands, smooth her hair with my hands, and think about the blood drying on her legs but don't move to get a cloth to clean her, because she needs me. Needs the glue from my hands so she won't crack. Sarah, please don't crack, don't crack! And she is silent, until she slips from my hands into sleep.

The wind dies down. The witches have nothing left to cackle about.

Sarah is so quiet in the house the next morning. Mother calls her "moody" to her face at breakfast, but Sarah just smiles a small smile and stares straight past her, like she doesn't even hear her, then pulls Panda out from under the table.

"See, Lettie put all the stuffing back and sewed Panda up good as new this morning, Emily." She holds the bear out for me to inspect. An invisible new seam runs down the bear's back.

"The mess, Emily, don't tell them about the mess," Sarah whispers nervously into my ear.

"Aren't you a bit old for bears, Sarah?" Father comes out from behind the newspaper that he's reading and looks over at Sarah for an instant, then disappears behind the paper again.

"Rather bears than boys, according to her gym teacher!" Mother, who's buttering thin toast, smirks, then adds, "I'm in the finals of our Ladies' Tennis Club today. Fancy that, girls, Lily Iris made it into the finals, fair and square!"

"There's a first for everything!" Father snorts, folding his newspaper up and peering level-eyed at Mother.

"Now, now, Bob. When was the last time you were in the finals of anything? Do tell." Mother tugs on her pearl earring.

Like a hollow Ping-Pong ball, their words bounce back and forth across the table. Their attention is fixed on who will win the game. They do not notice that Sarah has become like the Russian doll. Only I see that her eyes are painted in flat colors now and that her red lips are frozen open in a shocked O.

Peg and Jock

That evening they come with the news for Mother and Father. Father has just come home from his warehouse, and Mother is still smarting about having lost in her tennis tournament. Streak and Otis have not come out of the camping trailer all day, and Sarah went straight to her room after she got home from school. I tried several times to get her to let me in, but she sent me away, so I spent most of the afternoon with the kittens, who are weaned and playful, hoping that Streak would come to find me, but he never came, and I was too afraid to go near the trailer to call him. I held the kittens close, hoping that their fur would somehow warm me inside. I told them that things were bad, very bad, at our house right now, and it was good that they would soon be going to live somewhere else.

Mother and Father are seated opposite each other on the living room couches. I'm standing in the doorway, one foot in the passageway, the other in the room, when Peg and Jock come in.

"We won't be joining you for dinner tonight. Come to tell you that we're leaving right away, moving on."

"So sudden, why so—" Mother begins to ask, but Jock cuts her off.

"Job offer. *Cape Journal* needs a few months' work from me, is all. Need me there as soon as possible." Jock clenches his jaw and shuffles his feet in his sagging khaki trousers from one leg to the other. He catches my eye for a second then looks quickly away.

"Well, we're certainly pleased for you, Jock." Father coughs and stands up.

I look at Peg. Her eyes stare out hard as black marbles. She runs her hands up and down Opalina, whose tail twitches against her neck, then she takes a step in front of Jock. "We're sorry about the last minute of it all. We appreciate what you did for us. . . . It's time to move on, is all. Time to move on."

"What a shame!" Mother stands too. She seems genuinely upset. "The children will really miss each other, I'm sure. We've so enjoyed having you, haven't we, Bob?" For once Father agrees with her.

"Streak!" His name spills out of my mouth before I can even think. "Streak! I need to see Streak!" I race across the living room toward the front door, but Peg catches my arm sharply.

"NO!" she spits like vinegar at me. "No, Emily," she says softer this time. "It's not a good idea right now. Boys both seem to be sick or something. Flu came on strong, throwing up and all." She looks at Mother and Father, her thin lips twitching in rhythm with Opalina.

"Sorry, girlie," Jock reaches to touch the top of my head, like he did the first day I met him, but I duck away from his open palm.

"The kitten! I promised him the kitten!" I run from the room, run, with every crack holding together inside me, to the Cattery Club.

I find the kittens curled together, asleep in a dusty corner. They lie so tightly fitted against each other that I can't tell where one kitten's fur begins and another ends. Orange into white, gray into white, white into black, a fluffy ball of one. My hands ache as I pull the kittens apart and separate out the floppy gray and white body of No-Name.

"Courage, you will need courage," I pick Streak's kitten up and kiss it. "Streak will look after you. Streak will take good care of you! Be his friend, for me." I rub its soft fur against my cheek, then run with the sleepy kitten in my hands.

As I reach the top of the driveway, I hear the grinding sound of the Land Rover's battered engine starting up.

"No! No! Wait. Please!" I scream. The world turns at a strange pace, speeded up and slowed down at the same time. The gravel bites into my bare feet as I run down toward the camping trailer that's swaying on its wheels, hitched again to the Land Rover, as Jock starts to back it out of our driveway.

"Emily!" Mother and Father shout down to me from the veranda, their voices roll toward me slowly, a sound that seems to come from very far away.

Straight ahead, at the bottom of the gates, leaning against one white pillar is Buza, his wooden stick in his hand.

"Stop them, Buza! Don't let them through!" I yell.

In this moment, when the world is spinning away from me, I

see something cross into his old eyes as I race downward with the kitten bouncing in my hands.

Buza draws his chest up, raises his body as tall as he can, his head held high on his wrinkled, thin neck. The light catches his glowing earlobes and his eyes burn like two lit torches. Then like a Zulu warrior facing the gunpowder of the Boer army, Buza steps fiercely into the middle of the driveway and raises his stick in front of him.

"*Silo Sikazulu!*" He commands the Land Rover to stop, his voice loud and strong.

There is a roaring of gravel against tires as Jock brakes sharply. The Land Rover throws a cloud of dust around the back of the camping trailer, just inches away from Buza. He doesn't move.

"I could have killed you, you stupid old *kaffir!*" Jock leans out the driver's window and bellows at Buza as I slow my pace and slink past him to Streak in the trailer. "Just make it quick, girlie," Jock says grimly to me.

"I am not moving, Miss Emily." Buza keeps his stick raised in front of the camping trailer, which seems hypnotized by him and his magic stick to stay still, just like the chickens. In that instant I wish that I could keep the Land Rover still, stop them from taking Streak away from me if I don't clap my hands. "Magic, Miss Emily. You make magic," I hear Buza's voice echo inside me, when I clapped my hands and made the chickens flap and squawk.

Through the dirty window of the camping trailer I see Streak's face. Patchy and pale he stares out at me. He tries to open the window from the inside, but it only opens a little way. Streak puts his mouth to the crack in the window and whispers down to me. "Won't open any more, Em'ly."

"Open the door, Streak," I plead frantically.

"Can't. Pa's gone locked it with the key." Streak sniffs and stares at me.

"The kitten. I brought you your kitten!" I stand on my tip-toes while Streak reaches his fingers through the space in the window. The kitten mews softly as Streak tries to pull it in, but it's too big to fit through the tiny space.

"It ain't gonna work, Em'ly. Nothin's gonna work again. Pa, he beat Otis up so bad last night with the *knobkerrie*. He been moanin' an spittin' blood on his bunkbed all day. His face don't even look like a face no more. Otis did somethin' bad, Em'ly, real bad, didn't he?" Streak whispers hoarsely to me.

"Boy! You shut that window now, and let's get going! Had enough time to say good-bye to the little shiela!" Jock yells out his window and revs the Land Rover's engine up again, sending a cloud of exhaust fumes all around us.

"Take good care of my kitten, Emily." Streak's eyes fill up.

"Streak, you're my best friend." Tears stream down my face. "The only boy. . . ." I reach up to touch his fingers, feel the glue on my hands from his fingertips, as the trailer inches backward.

Through the dust haze, I look at Buza and nod that it's okay to let them pass. He slowly lowers his stick, then with a gentle movement of his hand, Buza salutes me. It gives me the strength to look up at Streak one last time. His fingers reaching, groping through the space in the window as they turn out of our driveway and onto the street. I stand at the bottom of the driveway with Buza and watch as they take the last bend in the road, strain to glimpse Streak's hand, which gets smaller and smaller until I can no longer see it. Listening until the tinny rattle of the Land Rover fades away completely, and disappears out of our lives.

Through blurred eyes I look first at Buza, then turn slowly toward the veranda where Mother and Father are still standing, like the two white pillars at the bottom of the gate, cemented into the ground on opposite sides of a path.

I hold the kitten close, its soft purrs blending with the sound of my crying, "No-Name. You will always be Streak's kitten," I sob into its fur, "and you will never have a name, because Streak says things that have names always go away. They always go away."

I feel Buza's hands on my shoulders. "Ay, Miss Emily. I will say that kitten is lucky it did not have to go with those *abathakathi*, the bringers of evil. Very lucky, Miss Emily." Buza's trembling fingers stroke the kitten's head. "You no worry about your friend. He will be all right. I sprinkled something on him once. *Inteleze*, war medicine to keep a warrior safe. Me, I knew he would need it."

A Package

I find it in the Cattery Club when I take No-Name back to the other kittens. It has been placed on the small chair where Streak sat that first time opposite me, his dirty fingers tugging at the hole in his shorts, the half-wilting violets between us. How long ago that feels now, so very long ago.

The package is wrapped in an old brown-paper bag. There is a scrap of white paper pinned to its outside. As I reach for it, I feel the hollow stillness inside me, see the trembling evening light on a spiderweb in the dusty corner.

At the bottom of the note written in blue ink is a name. "Peg." She must have put it there for me before they left, but I didn't see it, didn't fix my eyes on anything except the kitten that needed to be taken to Streak so urgently.

Here on the ground I read Peg's words. Words that spin around me tight, like the snake around her neck. Squeezing the air out of me so fast that my eyes blur on each letter.

Emily. Tell yor sister sorry. We dint mean harm to come.
May God help us all. Peg.

I punch at the brown-paper bag with my fists, feel the package burst open from the pounding of my knuckles. The faint smell of the fish and chips that were once wrapped in it comes up at me, forces the rings inside my stomach to squeeze a sick and greasy taste into my throat.

In the package is Sarah's nightgown. Pink and pressed. Neatly folded, like it is newborn, coming clean into the world for the first time. Stillborn in my hands, stinking of the dirty paper it was hidden in. There are no marks on it now from being pulled hard from her body. No sign of being held against Otis's nakedness. Nothing. Just a washed, pressed nightie that feels as soft and looks as pretty as ever.

I think how Sarah used to look in it, clean and powdered after a bath, her hair shining around her face and falling down her back. But not anymore. Now Sarah is buried on the inside, sewn up with an invisible seam like her panda bear. This is when pieces don't fit, when things start to float into crazy shapes in my head. I tear at the note, grind it up so small with my fingers and watch it float to the ground like white dust. Specks of nothing that no one will ever see.

I run past the servants' quarters, waving Sarah's nightie like a flag in the air, wanting to show her that it's clean and all better now. And maybe if she puts it on things will go back to the way it was before they came in their camping trailer. Before spring. Before Otis bloodied up my sister and her nightie.

Lettie stands on the path in front of me as I run toward the house. I try to get past her, almost toppling a metal bucket of soapy water that's balanced on her head, but she catches me firmly by the arm.

"Miss Emily, what is going on?" She looks sternly at me then fixes her gaze on Sarah's nightie in my hands.

My breath comes hard, my heart hurting on the inside. "It's Sarah's. I need to give it back to her," I pant.

"Where you find it, Miss Emily?"

"Somewhere." My teeth stick to the inside of my lips.

Lettie pulls me toward her. "This morning I find Madam Peg here in the back laundry room washing something. She get a big fright when I come in and see her bending on her knees over the washing board. She leave so fast, but I'm seeing the thing in her hand. Looks to me like Miss Sarah's nightie. Same nightie, no, Miss Emily?" Lettie moves her face close to mine and grips my shoulder. "You tell me what is going on, please."

"Lettie, I don't know. I can't say. I can't—"

"Miss Emily." Lettie holds my arm firmly, the bucket wobbling on her head. "I am feeling terrible inside. I say something no good happen here is why they leave so fast. After Madam Peg go from the washing room, leaving the floor all wet from the nightie dripping water from her hand. I see, when I go to wash the big tablecloth in the basin, I see red inside. Like blood." Lettie lowers her voice and looks at me, her eyes holding hard on mine. "It looks to me like blood, Miss Emily."

"Sarah's not doing too well. I promised her . . . Maybe if I give her back her nightie, maybe. . . ." I pull away from Lettie and bolt down the path leaving her standing alone with the bucket of water still fixed to her head. I run before I tell. Run with every part of me wanting to empty myself of the thing Otis did, but I can't. Won't, unless Sarah says so.

Sarah, I think as I stand outside her closed door, I will tell her about the note. About how sorry they are. How no one wanted to hurt her. But not the last part. Not the part about God.

Her curtains are closed. The room is dark like a cave and has the sweet damp smell of a place that's been shut up for a while.

"Sarah?" I see the hazy shape of her body on the bed. "Sarah, can I put the light on?" I step over the clothes that lie strewn across the floor.

"No," she whispers, her back turned.

"They're gone. I don't know if you know. They left."

Sarah coughs. Sniffs. Coughs again.

"Sarah. Peg left a note." I take a step closer to her bed. "Said how sorry she was. How they didn't mean harm to come."

Sarah lets out a ragged laugh. "Harm to come. Harm to come." She flings herself onto her back and covers her face with her hands. "I hurt, Emily. It hurts a lot inside."

I rub her foot gently with her nightie.

"What's that!" she pulls her leg away fast, curling it under herself.

"Your nightie. Peg left it for you. It's all washed and cleaned."

Sarah lunges at me so fast I don't have time to think. She knocks me to the ground, leans over me, her breath raspy and cold on my face. "Get it out of here, Emily. Get it away from me. Take it and bury it somewhere so I never have to see it again." Her fingers dig into my shoulders hard.

"Sarah," I sob. "Sarah please, you're hurting me, you're scaring me. Sarah, I'm sorry, so sorry."

She looks down at me, her eyes flat and empty. She crouches above me, grabs a discarded shoe, and throws it. Something crashes to the ground. "There!" she laughs harshly. "Now my room's a mess, Emily. Just like everything else!" From deep in her comes a hollow moan, a dark echo from inside her wound. She collapses onto me, and I feel her familiar shape, her long, thin arms and bony ribs. I suck in air through her matted hair, but the strands smell sour, like rotting fruit, and I pull my head away. Sarah's sweet marmalade smell is gone.

"It's everywhere," she whispers, her mouth close to my ear. "I tried so hard to keep it out." She rolls away from me onto her back and throws her arms out toward her littered room. "But see, it's no use, the mess. It's everywhere now."

It is between the mulberry bushes that I run to bury her nightie. On all fours I dig, like a frothy-mouthed dog, into the moldy soil. Earthworms slip between my fingers, red ants bite at my knuckles, but I don't stop until the hole is large enough to swallow up the nightie. With a ragged cry, I fling it into the gaping ground. Then I rip at my necklace, watch the glass angel as it floats through the air and lands on the dungeon of pink fabric. My throat closes as I toss the gold chain in after the angel. I hurl mud and leaves and twigs, and rake the earth over and over with my raw fingers. Seal it up, close up this shadowy place, don't stop until the nightie and necklace have disappeared and no one will ever find them again.

Sarah

Sarah brushes her hair and wears the same dresses and floral pinafores that she always wore. But wild strands escape from her ponytails, and spots of mayonnaise dot her clothes. Sarah doesn't seem to mind in the least like she would have before. She goes to school and comes home. Says she's studying with the door closed. Inside her room, the clothes have been put away, but not in any special order or pattern anymore. She answers Mother's and Father's questions, misty words through her hollow mouth. And I wait for her to laugh and to call me Em, but she doesn't. It's Sarah's shadow that lives in the house with us now.

"I'm going for a walk in the woods, Emily." Sarah comes by the Cattery Club, where I sit with the kittens folded into my lap like pretzels.

"Can I come with?" I ask.

"No. Panda's coming. I won't be long." She holds the bear by one arm, his floppy body hovering in midair. In her other hand is a shoebox. "I have something to give you, Emily." She holds out the box to me. "The new silkworms, I want you to have the whole slimy, wriggling lot."

"But, Sarah—"

"I can't stand the sight of them anymore, Emily." She leaves the box on the open windowsill of the Cattery Club. "I'm going for a walk now."

"Sarah. It's late. It's almost suppertime." I stand, spilling the kittens onto the floor.

"I won't be long." She bends to go out through the door, then turns to me and adds, "I thought Mother would be back by now. She must still be playing tennis."

"Yes," I say slowly, "she must still be playing tennis." I look into Sarah's eyes and wait for her to give me her special look that shows we both know that "tennis" means "Dennis," but Sarah turns away quickly and leaves.

I spend a long time in the Cattery Club, writing the names of each kitten and what they like to eat on cards for their new owners, who will be picking them up on the weekend. When the light gets too dim for me to write anymore, I know that Sarah has been gone longer than she said.

I find Lettie frying lamb chops in the kitchen for dinner.

"Lettie, please go find Sarah. She went into the woods and hasn't come back yet."

Lettie wipes the corner of her apron across her damp forehead and points the fork that she's using to turn the chops in my direction.

"Miss Emily, I would right now, but Baas Bob, he's coming

home anytime soon. You know how he complain if the supper is not ready." She turns back to the lamb chops, which are splattering oil across the stove top. "You go quickly to Buza, he doesn't have to make no meal for four people. You ask him to go look for Miss Sarah right away!"

I walk quickly down to Buza at the gates, past the spot where the camping trailer used to be parked. There is still missing gravel in the places where the tires rested and open spaces in the ground where the stairs that lead into it were placed. I think about the ocean, how it washes away sandcastles that have been left overnight on the beach, but there are no waves here to smooth away the holes that the gypsies have left.

As I come toward him, I see Buza's eyes are closed. His head bent forward, his chin resting on his folded, wrinkled hands, which cover the top of his stick.

"Yes, Miss Emily," he says without opening his eyes.

"It's Sarah. I'm worried about her. She went for a walk."

"Yes, I see her." Buza's gray eyelashes flutter open. "I say, 'Don't go far, Miss Sarah, night coming soon,' but she wave and keep walking." Buza rolls his stick between his palms. "You worry about Miss Sarah?"

I nod, feel my chest tighten.

"Me too, Miss Emily." He grinds his stick into the ground. "Sarah, she have a smile but no laugh. She have words but no voice. Sarah's spirit, I think it has left with the *dingiswayos,* the wanderers." Buza lifts his stick and points it toward the street and traces an imaginary line to the first bend in the road, where he and I had watched the camping trailer disappear.

Our eyes fix on that point for a moment, before Buza lowers the stick to the ground.

"Buza. Please go find Sarah. I don't want anything to happen . . ."

"I go right now, Miss Emily." He pushes his weight onto his stick and stands. "You no worry, I find her." I watch as he places one leg carefully in front of the other and walks slowly across the darkening street.

I stand at the edge of the road, throwing pieces of gravel into the middle of the street to keep myself busy. Mother's car headlights catch piece number one hundred sixty-nine in their beam as she turns into the driveway. She stops the car with a sharp jolt when she sees me on the side of the road.

"Emily, get back inside!" she yells out the window. "Honestly, you and your sister both need a good talking to. First Sarah, then you. Come on!" She waves for me to follow and puts her car into rapid motion. When we reach the parking spot Mother slams her door shut, then marches around to the passenger side and flings the door open.

"Come on, Sarah. Out!" She puts her hand on the waistband of her white tennis skirt and taps her foot.

"Sarah's with you?" I feel the tightness in my chest start to lift as I approach Mother's car.

"Yes, as it happens." Mother holds the car door open with her tennis racket and peers into the car. "I found her sitting on the side of the road at the other end of the lake, soaked to the knees, with that ridiculous panda bear on her lap. She won't talk to me and won't tell me what in God's name she was doing in the water." Mother squints one green eye at me and raises an eyebrow. "Maybe *you* know, Miss Waiting-on-the-Side-of-the-Road."

I push past Mother and reach into the car for Sarah, who's slid herself down into the seat and clutches Panda across her chest. I place my hand over hers, feel the chill of her skin through my palm.

"Sarah, I was so worried. Come, Sarah. Let's go inside." I coax her gently. She moves into my hands, soft and easy like one of the kittens.

She stands next to Mother's car for a second, then begins to move forward slowly, her body weaving from side to side.

"Jesus!" Mother kicks the car door shut with her tennis shoe so hard that the yellow pom-pom on the back of her sock bounces wildly against her heel. "If I didn't know better, I'd swear you'd helped yourself to some Scotch from the liquor cabinet. Girls, into the house now! I want to know what's gotten into you both. Sarah wet and a mile from home and you, Emily, out on the street after dark!" Mother marches swiftly up the veranda steps. I hold Sarah up, and we follow Mother's perfumed trail.

"Tell her, Sarah!" I whisper.

"Tell her what, Emily?" Sarah slurs.

"About Otis. About what he did."

Sarah tightens against me for a second at the mention of Otis's name, then relaxes. "I don't know what you mean, Emily," she says drowsily as we walk through the front door.

"Sarah, it's what made you this way. You must tell her!"

"I'm tired, Emily. I just need somewhere to sleep. I'll be fine after I get some sleep." She smiles sadly at me and pats my hand.

"It's just that beds bite sometimes, Emily, did you know?" She takes painfully small steps toward Mother, who's thrown her tennis racket onto the coffee table and has perched herself on the edge of one of the couches, her arms folded, her fingernails drumming a silent tune on the sleeve of her cotton blouse.

"Mother," Sarah says perfectly, suddenly seeming to come out of her daze, "I'm sorry for being out late, for getting wet. It won't happen again. It's all the late-night studying. I'm not hungry and need some sleep, so excuse me."

I think, just then, how much Sarah sounds like she always did before the thing with Otis happened. It makes me want to run over and smell her hair, to see if she's back, wanting so badly for it to be sweet-smelling again. But Sarah leaves the room humming a strange song, and I hear her bedroom door slam shut behind her.

"Well, well. That takes care of that." Mother runs a hand through her hair and leaves it resting on the side of her neck. "And you, Emily? What do you have to say about your bad behavior?" She eases her feet out of her tennis shoes and rotates her slim ankles around and around in circles.

"Tough game of tennis, Mother?" I ask, my lips quivering.

"Exhausting. Really played a rough set or two." She bends down and massages her foot with her hands.

I bite down hard on my lower lip.

"Well, I'm waiting for an apology or an explanation. Either will do just fine, Emily. Your sister opted for an apology, so what'll it be?"

"Neither, Mother." I stand in front of her, feel my body shaking all over, wanting to shove her hands away from her precious foot. "All you care about is playing tennis or whatever it is you do in the afternoons."

Mother snaps her head back. "I don't know what you mean by 'whatever it is I do,' Emily." She narrows her green eyes and bares her teeth like a panther at me.

"I mean, Mother, since Dennis is back in town, you seem to be playing an awful lot of tennis!"

"How dare you!" I feel the back of her hand sting hard across my face, feel the prickly surge of tears behind my eyes. "You shut your filthy little mouth! You hear?"

I cover my face with my hands. Watch my tears fall onto her tennis racket on the table and hope the salt will ruin its strings.

Lettie knocks timidly on the open living room door. "Excuse me, Madam."

Mother backs away from me, swivels around angrily, "Yes!"

"Baas Bob, I see his car in the driveway. The supper, it is ready."

"You can take Sarah's place away, Lettie. She's not hungry tonight." Mother turns to me abruptly. "Emily, go wash your face and come to the table. This conversation is over."

I have no more words inside me for her, and I do as I'm told.

🌿 🌿 🌿

Buza! I think suddenly as I splash cold water on my face. He must still be out looking for Sarah!

I hear the front door open and the thud of Father's briefcase as he puts it on the floor.

"What's the hurry, Emily?" Father says as I come running into the living room, the face towel still in my hands.

"Father, was Buza at the gates when you came in? Was he?"

"Emily, calm down. What's this all about?" He frowns then puts his hand to his chin. "Come to think of it, I didn't see the old man as I pulled in. What's this all about, then?" he asks again, undoing the top button of his shirt and sliding the tie out from under his collar. "Lettie, bring on the food. I'm starving!" he shouts toward the kitchen.

"Coming, Baas Bob, coming," her voice blotted out behind the rattling noise of dishes being gathered together.

"Father, Buza's still in the woods looking for Sarah. I have to tell him that she's okay, that she came back!"

"Just a second, young miss." Father holds his tie out between his hands in front of me blocking my way to the front door. "You're not putting one foot out that door. Buza knows how to take care of himself. He certainly won't melt in the dark, now, will he?" he adds as Mother, who's changed out of her tennis clothes, comes into the room.

"Where's Sarah?" Father snaps at her.

"In her room, Bob." Mother swings the belt tassels of her dress as she walks across the floor. "She's just not hungry, that's all. Let's go eat dinner like a nice, happy family, shall we?" she says using her smooth soft voice. Then she dips her head toward me and gives me a warning smile. "Right, Emily?"

"I want to know what the dickens is going on, Lily," Father says as we follow her to the table. "Emily says she sent Buza to look for Sarah or something?"

"Sarah just went for a walk a little too late. I found her and brought her home." Mother seats herself across the table from Father, while I stand behind my chair, not wanting to sit.

"Emily, aren't you a bit young to be instructing the servants; sending old Buza on a wild goose chase?"

"Mother wasn't here! It was late! Sarah was acting strange. I was worried. I really was!" I take Father's arm, look pleadingly into his eyes.

"Now, now, Emily." He pats the top of my hand lightly. "You've got yourself all upset over nothing. Sarah is home. The excitement is over. Let's sit down now and have dinner." He takes his hand from mine and ushers me to sit in the seat beside him. "Lettie! We're ready!" he shouts impatiently. "The woman is as slow as molasses," he grumbles to no one in particular, then looks over at Mother and adds, "Tennis ended later than usual, Lily?"

Before Mother has a chance to answer, Lettie, carrying a large tray with three steaming platters on it, appears in the doorway.

"Lamb chops, gem squash, and mashed potatoes, Baas Bob." She tells Father the evening menu as she does every night.

"Jolly good. Jolly good!" Father smacks his lips.

Lettie's eyes dart nervously from Mother to Father while she dishes the portions onto the plates. As she puts my food in front of me, I whisper to her, "Is Buza back?" She shakes her head, then disappears into the kitchen.

"Sarah seems to be in the thick of that difficult stage young girls go through." Father sprinkles salt onto his plate. "Seems to be spending an awful lot of time in her room doing homework. I'm glad she's at least taking school seriously."

"I'll have Lettie take her a plate of food." Mother wipes the side of her mouth with a napkin. "She does look a little pale. Seems to be having a hard time sleeping. I think I'll make an appointment with Dr. Hamilton for her." Mother spears a piece of meat onto her fork. "*Why* she has to have that old panda with her all the time, I *can't* understand."

"Why don't you ask her, Mother?" I say, pushing the food around my plate.

"I did, Emily." Mother looks smugly at me. "I think she's just being silly about growing up and not wanting to let go of childish things."

"She's a little old to be dragging a bear around, Lily. What'll her teachers think?" Father shrugs, then he sees Lettie at the door. "What is it, Lettie?" He taps the edge of the table.

"Baas Bob." Lettie twists her plump fingers nervously together.

"Yes, Lettie, speak up. Problem in the kitchen?"

"No, Baas Bob." She takes a step farther into the room. "My friend, Lena, she work three houses down. She comes now to me and says she hear from her other friend, who is working near Lakeside Police Station, she say to Lena, the old Zulu night watchman who works in the big house by the woods, he is caught without his passbook by the lake. The police, they arrest him and take him to the police station."

"Buza, no!" I leap from the table.

"Silly old man." Father throws down his napkin. "He should know better than to leave the house without his passbook!"

"It's all my fault! Father, it's not his fault. He went because I asked him."

"Calm down, just calm yourself, Emily." Mother puts a hand to her forehead. "This is easily solved. After dinner, Lettie will go to Buza's room and find his passbook, then Father will go and get him. Now sit down and finish your dinner. Emily, that's an order!"

"No!" I push myself away from the table, knocking the chair behind me to the ground. "We must go now! Father, please, let me come with you!" I pull him by the arm.

"Baas Bob," Lettie says softly, "after eight o'clock, they will take Buza to the Fort, downtown. I know. They do this one time to my cousin Samuel. They hurt poor Samuel very bad down there, Baas Bob."

"Okay, okay!" Father throws his hands up, pushes away his plate of unfinished food. "Go to his room and find the blasted thing!" He waves her out of the room. "Servants can be such a damn nuisance!" he mutters under his breath, as I run after Lettie to help her find Buza's passbook.

Bricks

They are stacked under the four iron legs of Buza's bed to keep away the *tokalosh*, the bad scary man, who, he has told me, might come and take him away in the night.

"How do the bricks keep the *tokalosh* from getting you?" I ask Lettie as she jerks open the wobbly drawers of the old night table next to Buza's bed.

"They say, if you are high up, the *tokalosh*, he cannot reach you. *Ay, Ay, Ay,* Miss Emily, where he keep his passbook?" Her large chest heaves fast, her fingers pull out bits of paper, an old snuff tin, a bead box from Buza's drawer.

I am frozen on the stone floor of his room, remembering when I first got my bike and rode it to the Lakeside shops. A police truck with bars on its small back windows passed by me. Circled slowly, like a shark about to make an attack, around three black gardeners as they lifted a lawnmower into the back of a van. I heard the rumble of their fear, the scraping sound of worn shoes racing away from the thick truck wheels. "The Black Maria, *ayzirorie!* The Black Maria!" the men screamed and scattered down the street, the lawnmower crashing to the ground as the police jumped from the van to catch them. And I kept pedaling, pedaling, pedaling.

I hold the copper bracelet Buza has left on his night table and imagine Buza's feet moving slowly through the woods, crackling blue gum bark under his smooth, hard soles. See the shiny, black boots of the policemen as they come toward him. Pointed boots facing his round, brown toes. See him reach painfully for his back as they force him to move quickly to keep up with them, then drag him into the Black Maria and drive away in the dark.

"If he was younger, if he could have climbed a tree, then maybe they wouldn't have got him, Lettie," I say as I go through the pockets of his old green coat that hangs on a hook on the wall.

"What crazy talk is this, Miss Emily!" she grunts, pulling up the worn rough woven blanket on Buza's bed and looking under the mattress.

"The police, they come and take you in the dark, like the *tokalosh*. If Buza had been higher up—"

"*Hayakona*, Miss Emily! You musn't let people hear you talk bad about the police, you hear? You get in a lot of trouble," she whispers. From under the *doek* on her head, sweat trails run across her brow. "The passbook, where he keep his passbook?" She turns her body around in circles in the small room.

I take a deep breath. I can smell the snuff from Buza's hands, the night earth from his old clothes, the camphor oil that he rubs on his knees, even the old-wood scent of his stick. Lettie stands so close to me in the small space, but it is only Buza who is with me in the room.

"Get him back, Lettie, we've got to get him back!" I cry. "Why do you have to carry stupid passbooks, anyway?"

"The law, Miss Emily. It says us black people must have a passbook with us all the time. It give us permission to live in a place, otherwise they take us to jail." She wipes the sweat that's run down her neck with the palm of her hand, then looks around the room anxiously. "Help me now, Miss Emily. Look there, under the picture." She points to a wooden box against the wall. On the box are Buza's *muthi* tins. I move the tins carefully and feel the special medicines that he keeps inside them shift about.

I look up at the picture on the wall above me. The photo of the girl, maybe a few years older than Sarah, standing in the veld, a *doek* covering her head, a plain white blouse, and a too-big skirt falling over her skinny legs. A round hut in the background, a naked baby balanced in the crook of her arm.

"The girl in the picture," I point to her smiling face, "that's Matilda."

"Yes, that is Matilda." Lettie, balancing on her knees, rummages through the wooden box at my feet, then looks up. "Buza's daughter, his only child. The baby, Ezekiel, he is Buza's grandson. Did he tell you, they are living in Zululand? Buza, he has not seen her in a long time. The baby," she laughs sadly, "he will probably be a big boy before Buza sees him."

I run my fingers over Matilda's picture. See how close she holds the baby, how big her smile is. I think of all the bracelets

Buza has placed in my hands and all the stories he has told me and wonder how far Zululand is from Johannesburg.

"Here it is! Here it is! Old Buza, he keep his passbook in this empty *muthi* tin!" Lettie holds up a small, faded brown book. "Come, Miss Emily! Quick! Before they take him to the bigprison downtown. Buza, he is too old to go there. Is no good place for an old man." She takes my hand in hers. "Is no good place for anybody," she whispers.

Lakeside Police Station

A gray cement building that I pass every day on my way to school. It stands on the corner of Rhodes Avenue and Livingstone Road, just a block from the Lakeside shops and Mr. Pestano's greengrocery store and the movie theater where Sarah and I saw *My Fair Lady* and *The Sound of Music*. A building, just a building. I never thought about what went on inside. Never knew until tonight.

"I should have insisted that you stay home, Emily," Father says as we pass three Black Maria police trucks parked outside the police station.

We climb the steps leading into the gray building. Two bright lights shine down onto the front door, and we are suddenly spotlighted in their white glare, like two rabbits caught in the headlights of an unexpected car.

I look up at Father, who is shifting his jaw from side to side, grinding his teeth one against the other. He drums the brown leathery cover of Buza's passbook against the side of his leg as we walk up to the long wooden counter.

A clock on the wall says ten minutes to eight. Behind the

counter are two policemen. Father approaches them. I stand silently behind him and squint up at the policemen's blue jackets.

"Excuse me, Constable," Father says.

"*Sergeant.* Sergeant Grobbler," the policeman with the wide mustache and black slicked-back hair says to Father. "*Ya, meneer,* what can we do for you?"

"My name is Bob Iris, and I'm here to pick up my servant Buza. I believe he was arrested earlier tonight because he didn't have his passbook with him." Father says each word clearly in his most proper-sounding English, then places Buza's passbook on the counter.

"*O, ja.*" Sergeant Grobbler reaches a ruddy hand out and flips through the worn book, "Him and a whole mess of other domestics were picked up today." He turns Buza's passbook over in his hands, then lifts it to his nose. "Smells funny. Sweet like—" He frowns and hands it to the blond policeman next to him. "De Villiers, smell this. Tell me if you don't think it has a funny smell."

The younger policeman runs a big hand through his bristly crew cut and smiles. "I can always smell *dagga.* My nose is trained to sniff out drug-smoking *kaffirs.*" He holds Buza's passbook inches from his broad red nose.

"That's absurd!" Father raises his voice. "Buza is an old Zulu night watchman who's been with our family for years. Never in all his time with us have I ever seen him smoke as much as a cigarette!"

"*Meneer.*" Seargent Grobbler touches the corner of his black mustache and looks seriously at Father. "We aren't accusing your boy of anything. We're simply doing our job. You have to admit, it does have a strange smell." He snatches Buza's passbook from Constable de Villiers and holds it toward Father's nose.

"I hadn't noticed any smell," Father mumbles.

"The smell's from his *muthi* tin," I blurt out loudly. "Buza keeps his passbook in one of his medicine tins."

Father and the two policemen stop what they are doing and look down at me.

"A little English *meisie* with a very big voice." Sergeant Grobbler peers his dark head over the countertop, "What's your name, *meisie*?"

"Emily," I say quietly. "Emily Iris."

"Clever girl to know where your Zulu boy keeps his passbook."

"Lettie found it when we were looking in his room—"

"You go into the servant boy's room, *meisie*?" Constable de Villiers asks, tapping the point of his pen on Buza's passbook that Father has placed back on the counter.

"Sometimes," I whisper.

"Emily, I've told you a dozen times you're to stay away from the servants' quarters!" Father says gruffly.

"Mister Iris," Constable de Villiers rubs the tip of his broad nose with his hand. "You should keep a better watch on the whereabouts of your child, don't you think? Cavorting in the back rooms with the servants—"

"Look, gentlemen," Father says impatiently, "it's late. I have my servant's passbook, give me whatever there is to sign, and let's get on with it, shall we?"

"The temper of an Englishman," Constable de Villiers winks at Sergeant Grobbler. "Always ready to do battle." He flicks his pen across the countertop, and it spins toward Father. Then he hands Father some papers to sign.

"After you, *meneer,*" Sergeant Grobbler says when Father's done signing. He opens the swinging gate for Father to go through, then he turns to me. "Coming, *meisie?*"

Father is about to shake his head, but I slip through the gate before he has a chance to say no.

"Take them to the back." Sergeant Grobbler motions to a doorway behind him.

"Gladly." de Villiers stands and shakes his pants, smoothes down his blue jacket, and swaggers in front of Father. "Shall we?" he says in a fake-sounding English accent, imitating Father.

"Yes," Father says abruptly.

Constable de Villiers leads us down a corridor.

In the pale light, I see bleached green walls, stripped of their color, like the plants we put in a closet for a week without sunlight in biology class. We pass two closed doors on each side of the passageway. I walk close behind Father, who follows Constable de Villier's bouncing blond head. He brings us to a sudden stop in front of the last door on the right. From inside I hear a dull crunching sound. The smashing of something hard against something soft. A smothered moan. De Villiers opens the door and barks into the room.

"Pieterson! Get that *bliksem kaffir* off the floor and into the yard with the others. *Maak gou!* It's almost eight!"

A man. In the quick second that the door is opened I see him. Brown young hands laced like a flimsy dark doily over his black hair. He is on the floor curled up small, but not small enough to escape the boot that is pressed against his cheek.

I touch my own cheek. Rub my hand across it and imagine the pain of a boot against it. I think of a kudu antelope stumbling across the veld away from the jaws of a Cape hunting dog that bites chunks of jagged flesh from its weakening legs. Run, there is still place to run in the open bush. Here there is only a closed door shut tight on the whimpering man. I hold my own safe face with my shaking hands as we move on.

"Jesus Christ," Father whispers under his breath.

We follow Constable de Villiers into an empty waiting room at the end of the hallway. It is lit with white fluorescents above that make me blink until my eyes get used to the sudden hardness of light. There are no windows, no furniture. On the far wall is a door with a sign that says:

YARD / JAART

NO ADMITTANCE / GEEN TOEGANG

"Wait here." Constable de Villiers says, cocking his head toward Father. "I'll free your Zulu boy." He snort-laughs and moves away from us.

I can smell the sourness of the room. Sweat and moldy disinfectant mixed with stale, trapped cigarette smoke . . . and something else. Something I've feared so much. The feeling of being in an empty place with no air or sunlight, like the inside of Opalina's long snake stomach.

"Oh, lord!" Father groans, looking at the far wall.

I turn in his direction, see what he is seeing.

The ugly pattern of marks on the green wall. It starts near the baseboard and runs halfway up to the ceiling. From as high as a man's head to as low as his ankles, and everywhere in between. In the glare of the sickly whiteness that shines from above I see the stamped shapes of boot marks. Dark, heavy undersole imprints that have missed their target, out of control, like the skid marks of a car across a wet road.

"You shouldn't have come, Emily. Dammit, you shouldn't have come!" Father holds his hand over my eyes for an instant, then takes it away and shoves it back into his suit pocket. He knows that it is too late. The boot prints are scalded into my head already.

Constable de Villiers's bellowing voice breaks through the closed door so suddenly that Father and I both snap around and turn in the direction of the door. "Buza Vilakazi! Your *baas* is here for you. Move it, boy! Hey you, Retief, get the rest of the lot ready!"

I hear the sound of feet moving. No words, only silent shuffling, then a command shouted by a different police voice: "*Kom, julle kaffirs*, let's get going now!"

Father coughs, looks away from me.

More rustling from behind the door. Then a single sound reaches my ear. The low rumbling voice from deep inside someone. One voice becomes two, then three, then four, then many. Low, strong sounds coming together from behind the door. I hear them, their notes blending one into the other like angel voices in the dark, and I imagine their cold skin and the dark night air on their tired black faces.

"They're singing, Father."

"I hear them, Emily. I hear them," Fathers rubs the crease between his eyebrows just as the door is flung open.

"Buza," I say under my breath, and my body trembles.

He stands beside Constable de Villiers. His head is lowered, his rough work shirt pulled to one side showing his naked shoulder, his khaki shorts stained with mud. He holds his handcuffed wrists out toward de Villiers, who jangles keys like bait in front of him. Buza lifts his eyes and looks at me as de Villiers uncuffs him. Muddy old eyes, pools of still liquid that fill me up inside, make me burn with a longing to bite de Villiers so hard on the leg, bite into him until every tooth in my mouth comes out on his steel skin.

"Buza!" I run to him, want to feel his warm palm on my head, but he raises his hand up to stop me before I reach him. And I am frozen between Father and the boot marks on the wall, and the brightness of the room, and the laugh of de Villiers—and Buza, a crumpled warrior without a spear, for his stick is gone.

"Sarah? Miss Sarah?" Buza looks anxiously from Father to me.

"Home. She's all right," Father says, taking a step between de Villiers and Buza. "Was it really necessary for you to handcuff an old man?" he hisses at de Villiers through his teeth.

De Villiers digs his heels back and swings the handcuffs that are now free from Buza's wrists back and forth. "*Meneer* Iris." His pale eyes sear into Father's face. "Your Zulu boy broke the law. He should know better than to be out on the streets without a passbook doing God knows what." De Villiers raises his voice and points his hand that dangles the handcuffs at Buza. "Shouldn't you, boy?"

I watch Buza's shoulders hunch forward, his eyes lower to the ground. "Yes, *baas*, yes, *baas*," he says softly, bowing slightly in the direction of de Villiers.

"Now, take your boy and get out of here, *Mister* Iris!" de Villiers says curtly to Father.

Outside I take big breaths of the cool night, but the air sticks in my chest, and I feel the sky pressing down on us from above. The sidewalk next to the police station is empty now. The trucks have gone, with the angel voices locked inside them.

No-Name

The other kittens have gone to their new homes, and we are alone now.

I sit on the front lawn while No-Name sleeps on my lap. Big white paws folded over his soft gray nose. He doesn't know what might have been. Chasing rabbits in the Kalahari Desert. Hearing the hoot of a Cape owl in the Tsitsikamma forest. Curling up next to Streak on his bunkbed. Maybe. Or maybe things much worse.

"Streak. Where is he, No-Name? Where is he?" I think how much I need to tell him. How Sarah hides in her room and inside herself now. How Buza lost his stick somewhere in the woods, and even though we looked for it all afternoon yesterday, we couldn't find it. How watery Buza's eyes get when he stands with nothing to lean on, and how very slowly he walks without its rounded top to hold on to. But Streak is gone.

"Buza's making a new stick, No-Name." I stroke his belly, and he rolls over, opens his slate eyes, and looks up at me. "No-Name, if you were acting strange, not drinking your milk or bouncing around, wouldn't your mother notice?" No-Name licks my finger. "My mother's too busy, and Sarah, I don't know, she seems to have forgotten how she got to be like this. Mother's still so angry about what I said." I stroke his soft fur. "You're lucky mother cats don't play tennis." I let him down onto the ground. He mews loudly, then follows me to where Buza sits at the bottom of the gates, carving his new stick from a blue gum branch.

He holds a small carving knife in his hand and balances the bent branch between his legs. "Hard work, Miss Emily. Long time before it is finished. This is why a good stick should last forever." He brushes the bits of wood shavings from his bare legs. As he carves, the copper bracelets on his wrists separate from each other, and I see the rings of red welts that the hand-cuffs left on his paper-thin skin.

"Does it hurt, Buza," I ask softly, "your wrists?"

"Not here," Buza holds his wrist. "Here." He places an unsteady hand over his heart.

"I'm sorry."

"It's okay. I am all right. But, Miss Emily, Baas Bob, I think he will tell me go find another job. I make a big trouble with the passbook for him at the police station." Buza holds my gaze.

"If you go, I'm coming with you," I say fiercely. "Me and No-Name."

"Miss Emily, you are a funny one." Buza laughs, and his wrinkles soften around his eyes. He holds the stick out toward me and hands me the knife. "You help me carve this stick, Miss Emily, my fingers are too tired. It will be good for your hands to be on the stick to make it a good one. A mighty one. As mighty as the one my grandfather made me!"

I take a seat at his feet and feel the warmth inside that his words give me. A breeze comes off the lake, and I watch as the last of the jacaranda blossoms are scattered across the driveway. I hold the knife and cut into the branch with smooth, flat strokes, feel the curve of its bark against my skin, glad that I am a part of turning the branch into a walking stick that he will have forever.

"This will be your grandson's one day, Buza, won't it?" I say.

"Yes, my grandson." Buza sighs.

"The photo in your room. I looked at it when I helped Lettie find your passbook. Matilda, your daughter. You must miss her a lot."

"I do, Miss Emily. Yes, I do." He rubs his hands over the welts on his wrists, looks out across the road beyond the woods, and shakes his head.

"The singing at the police station, Buza. What were they singing?" I cut off a knobbly piece of bark.

Buza is silent for a moment. He takes out his snuff tin and shakes the black powder into his palm. "They were singing 'Nkosi Sikelel' iAfrika.'" It is a song asking God to bless Africa and to raise up our spirits. Strong. It makes them strong inside." He evens out the snuff in his palm with his finger. "They take the singing deep inside. It makes them feel as one." He inhales the snuff and reaches for a rag from his pocket. "Like glue, Miss Emily. The voices, they are like glue that keeps them together." He rubs his hands on the rag.

"Like Ma-we's egg," I say.

"Yes, Miss Emily. Like Ma-we's egg." He smiles down gently at me.

I feel the afternoon sun beat down on my back, hot and strong, and know that spring is almost over.

Early Morning

In the half light, I am jolted awake by the piercing sound of Lettie. High like a whistle she screams, *"Ay, ay, hayakona, hayakona!"*

Eyes still smeary with sleep, I throw myself out of bed and press myself against the bedroom window. Lettie. I see her running up the driveway, stumbling, her shoes and apron covered with green slime from the lake. She wrenches the *doek* off her head. Her gray-black hair cropped short underneath, startling me. I've never seen her head uncovered before.

Suddenly an ambulance bursts up the driveway, throwing gravel in all directions. Its back doors are opened by two men in white.

Out they come. Mother, green all over her cream silk robe, slime frosting in her hair, muck sliding between her bare toes, no shoes on her feet. Doesn't look like Mother. Mother doesn't look like that.

Now Father, hovering, leaning forward, hands crisscrossed over a stretcher that the two men in white carry out.

A shape under the sheet.

"Sarah! Sarah!" the voices scream together. The voice of Mother. The voice of Father. The voice of Lettie. The voice of me.

I am outside now.

"Emily!" Mother's voice, like a goose being strangled. "A terrible accident. . . . She left the house early this morning . . . went to the lake. . . . The weeds trapped her in the water, pulled her down. Oh, my God, she drowned! Help me!" She falls to the ground in front of me. "Help me!"

I don't move. Don't touch her.

Thoughts pound hard against my eyes from inside my head as the men in white lower the stretcher to the ground. A mistake. This is a horrible mistake. Sarah's in her bed sleeping.

Then a tangle of wet red hair falls out from under the sheet, and Panda rolls out of her clutched white hand.

"No, no!" I scream.

"Why take my Sarah? Why?" I hear Father's voice against the soaked sheet.

"Father!" I pull on the back of his shirt.

"She waded in the water, went a little too far . . . yelled for help and then got sucked down. . . . The boatman . . . couldn't find her in all the thick green muck until it was too late!" he wails, his knuckles showing even whiter than the sheet.

"Dear God, help me, Emily!" Mother's Flaming Scarlet nails scrape against my foot.

I take a step back. "No!" I scream, kicking gravel into Mother's face, the pieces, like shattered rock candy sticking to her hair, "You didn't see her . . . hear her . . . never did, never could!"

"Sarah! No!" Father is on his knees in front of the stretcher, holding on to Sarah and won't let her go. I think how Father never held her so close before.

"I want her!" I scream, ripping at Father's body, pulling him off Sarah, batting his desperate arms away from My sister, My sister, My Sarah, My Sarah.

Father falls toward Mother. They collapse together on the ground, rocking each other back and forth.

I lie across Sarah. Feel her so still under the sheet. My fingers catch in her matted, wet hair. I imagine her mouth, soft again, her eyes no longer flat. I breathe her in, press my nose up against her skin so hard, reaching in to her to find her sweet marmalade smell. I hold her icy fingers and press my lips against her cheek.

"Don't take her away!" I hear Mother scream to the men in white. "In the house! I want my daughter in the house!"

The men carry us, Sarah and me, inside.

Strange, disinfectant-smelling hands try to pull me from her as they lay the stretcher down on our living room floor. Her dampness seeps into me, fills me with the cold lake. I empty warm tears on her, wanting so badly to melt her iciness, pour hot honey glue on my sweet sister to heal her and bring her back to me. But Sarah's coldness and emptiness have been in her too long.

"Take me with you, Sarah!" I sob. "Don't leave me behind!" I rip the sheet from her, lay myself skin to skin on her, clutch her so tight, try to wriggle myself into her stone still body.

"No! No! NO!" I scream.

Warm, familiar hands reach for me. Rosewater smell and soft touch, cooing sounds like a mother to its lost baby bird, then fingers that pry me gently, slowly, limb by limb from my sister. "Come, Miss Emily, you hold on to me." Lettie's comfort voice and soft, cushiony body wrap around my limp form.

I hold on to Lettie for two days and nights. I sleep in the servants' quarters in her bed set on bricks and cry against the rough, thin blanket that covers us both. She rubs chamomile oil on me to try to calm the ache inside and sings me Xhosa lullabies through her own falling tears.

> *Thula thul' mntwana thula sana, thula san',*
> *Kuho abantu abanijongileyo, abanijongileyo.*

She sings to me over and over again in a voice that's deep and choked with sadness. Sometimes she sings so that I can understand the words, although I do not ask, do not speak, do not move from the safety of Lettie's touch and gaze.

> *Thula thula,* hush child, hush baby, hush baby,
> There are people watching over you, watching over you.

She helps me rest my head from thoughts of Sarah for a few minutes with word pictures of herself from when she was a young girl.

"My family, Miss Emily, they come to Johannesburg when I am nine from the Transkei. We lived in Soweto in a shanty house with one room. My small brother, Thomas, he was very sick from cold that first winter. We have no heat and no warm water to make him some hot soup for his sickness. Lucky for us, a nice white doctor from Baragwanath Hospital, he see Thomas selling newspapers at night on the streets with nothing warm on his shaking body, and he take Thomas in his car and give him a warm sweater and some medicine right away. He tell Thomas that he has a son same age as Thomas, and he even bring Thomas back in the car to our shanty house. *Ayzirorie!* The only white people that come into Soweto, they are the doctors and nurses and police. My family, we are so lucky that Dr. Greenberg, he found us and he look after us. *Hai!* After that, my mother, she went to work for Dr. Greenberg's family in their house in Dunkeld; and me, I take care of my brothers and sisters in Soweto—we four children. My mother, she only had Thursday afternoons and every second Sunday off to visit us—same as me now."

Lettie talks to me until my eyes close and sleep carries me to Soweto, a place I will never see. Then my dreams carry me back to Sarah. To a sister I will never see again.

Mother and Father don't come to get me from the off-limits servants' rooms. Now that everything is broken, their rules don't matter anymore, and they are left alone together in the big empty house without Sarah and me.

"Sarah is watching over you. Her lips are smiling just for you," Lettie whispers to me in the dark on the night before the funeral. "You must go back after tomorrow to Baas Bob and Madam Lily. They are needing you now." She holds me tight and kisses me gently on my forehead just before dawn comes.

Funeral

After the funeral, when the visitors are gone, I pass Mother and Father as they sit alone in the living room.

Mother's hair is pulled back tight from her temples, her face pale and without makeup. I remember how she once sat in front of her vanity table and rouged her high cheekbones and told Sarah and me, "When you are grown women, girls, never go out in public without makeup, even if it's only to the mailbox." But today in front of everyone, Mother doesn't seem to care who sees her naked face.

I cross the living room, hear the sound of Lettie crying as she clears away the teacups and cake plates from the dining room table.

"Tap, Father," I say. "You need to tap."

His arm rests on the back of the sofa behind Mother and a cigarette with a forgotten ash tip burns in his fingers.

He turns his unshaven face toward me. "Tap?" A puzzled, vacant expression crosses his shadowy face. "Oh, the cigarette. Yes. Thank you, Emily," he says quietly.

"I'm going to Buza at the gates," I tell them.

"Don't be gone too long, Emily," Mother says in a thin voice.

Sarah, can you see them? I think as I throw stones in the dark across the driveway. *Mother and Father sitting close together on the couch. Sarah, they held hands so tight together at your funeral, you couldn't separate them at all.*

Dennis, he was there, Sarah, but Mother just shook his hand and let him kiss her on the cheek. Mother didn't seem to notice anybody, Sarah. You see, Mother looked only at one thing the whole afternoon. Her eyes never left you, Sarah. Never left you in your box on the ground. Not once. Not once.

"Miss Emily, is that you?" Buza shines his flashlight in my direction. The light catches the tips of my black patent-leather shoes that Lettie had stretched out earlier with her hands so they wouldn't pinch during the funeral. But they pinched anyway, and the tiny sharp pinpricks bit into me all over like angry red ants under my skin.

"Miss Sarah," Buza says her name slowly to me and takes my hand in his, "she is in a good place. A very happy place."

I look at him through marbled red eyes, scrape my shoes against the gravel, feel the scratching of the petticoat under my dress.

At the graveside, when they said prayers and sprinkled rose petals over the coffin, I could hear Sarah's voice: "A dress! Goodness, Emily, this must be a very special occasion for you to be wearing a dress!" Her laughter tingled wildly inside my head with the memory of Sarah playing checkers with me and walking in the woods and talking about the perfect boy she was going to marry one day, making me dizzy with the sweet sound of Sarah . . . Sarah before Otis.

When they lowered her coffin into the ground, I imagined Panda resting on her chest, strands of her long red hair tangled around his damp fur. I demanded that Panda go with Sarah in the coffin, but Mother was worried that his fur was wet and would start to smell. "Sarah would have wanted it that way, Mother!" I screamed at her, and she fell back into a chair, wispy as a feather, and began to weep.

"Here. Drink, Miss Emily." Buza holds a tin mug toward me. "Strong *muthi*. I mix for you myself to make you strong again after someone die."

I take a sip and taste the thickness of wet soil and bark in my mouth. "Funny taste," I say through grimy teeth.

Buza rubs his knuckles. "Old Zulu custom, roots, *amakhubalo*, blue stones, bark and special black powder. It help, Miss Emily, it help." He pats me gently on the back and sighs, then he leans down and shines his flashlight on the ground between us. "Here is Sarah." He places a hand in the light of the beam. "And here is you and Master Bob and Madam Lily." He moves his hand and places it on the ground outside of the light. "My people, we say the person who die is in a special new place. And the people still left, they are in a new place too. Everything different, everything change for them too."

"Yes, Buza," I say quietly, "Everything is different." I take my hand and hold it in the path of the lightbeam. "Sarah," I cry, "Sarah!"

"Tears in the *muthi* cup is good. Make it even stronger. You cry, Miss Emily. You cry." He pauses, then says softly, "I tell my own child, Matilda, when her mother die, is good to cry."

"How old was she, Buza?" I sob.

"Eight. She only a small child when my wife die. My sister, she take care of Matilda after that."

"Have you ever made someone a promise and then wished you never had?" I cry so hard, gulping for air.

"Oh, yes, Miss Emily." Buza nods his head slowly. "I make a promise to my wife when she was very sick. Me, I was wanting to be home with her. To take care of her, but she knew I would lose my job if I came back home. She said, 'Buza, I am dying. It make no difference now. What is important is that you stay in Johannesburg and make enough money to send Matilda to school.'" Buza sighs and rubs his palms together. "I make her a promise to stay at my job, even though my heart, it hurt me very much. I went home only for a few days. Just for her funeral. I did what she asked. It is this that gives me peace inside. I kept my promise to her." Buza smiles softly, "You see, Miss Emily?"

"Yes." I say, drying my eyes. "Sarah. She had a secret. I made a promise not to tell Mother and Father. I never told them when she was— It's burning inside me, Buza, making holes inside my stomach."

"Then you must tell, Miss Emily. Is no good not to tell now."

We sit in the darkness and listen to the night bellow of a buffalo that comes from the zoo across the lake. Buza points with his new stick to the moon above. "Half slice, Miss Emily, is still only half slice."

"Does the sky look the same in Zululand?" I ask.

"No, Miss Emily. For me, the stars in Zululand, they are a little brighter." He tilts his head up toward the sky, then adds, "But maybe is because my family is there."

"Why can't you go home Buza?"

He shakes his head and lets out a soft whistle from between his teeth. "Not so easy, Miss Emily. Me, I need money to help Matilda. She be a nurse soon. Matilda's baby, he need money too for food." Buza looks over at me. "Is okay, is okay, Miss Emily. You not worry about me." He pats me gently on the shoulder. "You have much sadness now. I tell you a good story to help with the darkness inside you. Sit now, Miss Emily, sit." Buza stands and offers me his stool. "You not dirty the nice dress on the ground."

I pull myself onto Buza's wooden stool, while he leans on his new stick beside me.

"In a small Zulu village, Miss Emily, live a man and a woman who have two daughters, Yaphansi, the firstborn, and Intombi, the little one. The sisters, they love each other very much. Always laughing together on the bank of the River Shingwezsi and making small animals from the clay. They be sisters first, but good friends, as well."

"Like Sarah and me." I feel the petticoat netting, prickly against my legs.

"Just so, Miss Emily, just so." Buza continues, "Now, one day while Yaphansi and Intombi were sitting by the river, uGungqu, the river monster, he was floating in the river, close to where the girls were. He look at Yaphansi with his big ugly eyes and saw inside her, how good she was in her heart, how beautiful she was outside."

"How could he see inside her, Buza?"

"Can always see inside someone, Miss Emily." Buza taps his stick against the side of the stool. "What you have to do before you cross a road, Miss Emily?"

"Stop, look, listen," I say.

"Same thing with people, Miss Emily, same thing. uGungqu, the river monster, he lie still in the water. He see how gently Yaphansi use her hands, how sweet her voice to her sister is." Buza moves in a slow circle around me. "Now, when the sun start to go down over the hills, and Yaphansi reach into the water to wash the clay from her hands, uGungqu, he jump up and drag her under the water with him, wanting to take her goodness for himself."

"Oh, no!" I cry.

"Miss Emily, no worry!" Buza says quickly. "Look! The river creatures, the fishes and crabs, they see what is happening, and they come quickly to save Yaphansi. They swim so many onto uGungqu, their colors so bright in his eyes that he get blinded by them all, and they take Yaphansi from his sharp jaws. And Yaphansi, she stay under the water with the shiny fishes and crabs."

"The little sister, what about her, Buza?"

"She is crying and running fast back to the village, waving her hands full of red clay in the air. And the chief and all of the village, they went back to the river to find Yaphansi, but they cannot find her. And little Intombi, her heart is full of sadness, and every day she go to the river to look for her sister. But listen, Miss Emily," Buza stands in front of me, his eyes wide and open, "One day, while Intombi is looking into the water, she see the face of Yaphansi, and she beg her sister, 'Please Yaphansi, come back, come back. I am so sad without you.'"

I hold the stool on both sides with my hands so tight that they hurt, "What did she say, the sister in the river, Buza? What did she say?"

"Yaphansi, she say to her small sister, 'I am happy in the river with my friends of the water. It is quiet and beautiful here. You, my young sister, you must go back to the village and live and be strong.'" Buza leans his stick on the side of the stool and takes both my hands in his and looks softly into my eyes, "Then the big sister, she say, 'And when you are lonely, come sit by the river, look deep in your own heart. Inside you find much love and great strength. There you will find me, my beloved little sister.'"

I feel my tears spill onto his wrinkled hands, "What happened to Intombi, Buza?" I whisper.

"Intombi, she was a great Zulu, Miss Emily. She went from the river, and she laughed and she sang and she was happy all her life, for she never forgot her sister's words." Buza places my two hands together between his palms. "She was strong, and she had courage." His voice crackles softly. "Like you, Miss Emily, like you."

Mother and Father

I leave Buza at the gates and go inside to set Sarah's secret free.

Sarah. Otis. Bed. Blood.

Crumpled pieces of Mother and Father are scattered about the living room. Like two chameleons, I watch them change before my eyes.

"Emily! Why didn't you tell us! If only we had known sooner!" Father's hands rake through his thinning hair.

"You should have noticed, you would have known!" I spin like a top from him to her, her to him. "Stop, look, listen, Father! Stop, look, listen, Mother!" I point both hands in opposite directions.

Mother is stretched out on the floor, her arms holding the cushions of the couch, her silk robe splayed out behind her, like a wounded swan. "Oh, Sarah!" Mother wails. "She felt dirty. My darling girl went to the lake to feel clean again. She didn't want to die!"

"Lily." Father kneels beside her, places a hand on her back.

"Why didn't we . . . what was going on, we didn't see?" He traces a line with his hand along the rug. Then a hard sound comes from him, a raking of his voice against his heart, his body quivering.

"Busy! Too busy!" I scream. "Tennis, Mother, always something else! Work, Father! Your stinking chocolates. I hate them, did you know, I hate them!" I spit out at him, then turn to face them both. "People, always people living in our house. Never just us, never good enough just us!" I sob.

I am the blows of a *knobkerrie* against a body, the jaws of a lion on the neck of an impala. I hear the crumbling sounds that come from Mother and Father, hear my words, like the ragged teeth of a wild animal, ripping into their flesh.

Their hands reach for me, try to comfort me, but I curl into a ball so small and tight on the ground, like an egg, whole and complete. Like Ma-we's egg, I tell myself, like Ma-we's egg.

There is so much quiet in the house in the days that follow. Even the smallest sentences that are spoken between us hang in the air like fragile chandeliers.

Mother unplugs the phones. "No calls." She coils the extension cords tight around her hand, then drops them into a paper bag like they're dead snakes. "The ringing gives me a headache." I watch as she makes her way down the hallway, holding on to the walls for support.

Mother, I think, has no headache. She wants the phones disconnected because of the people calling with questions, wanting more, and Mother has nothing more to give except her horror and pain. Now the phones are switched off, and the people are gone as long as she can't hear them ringing inside her head. Even Dennis.

At school there are whispers in the hallway when I pass by.

"Her sister, Sarah, was found dead in the lake."

"Cut up in pieces like the other one?"

"No, it wasn't a murder. An accident. Drowned. Same like what happened to poor Marcy Le Roux two years ago. When the waterweeds are too big an' strong, they can take you down. . . ." Their hushed voices leap out at me.

"Let us take a minute to pray silently for Emily and her family," Miss Erasmus says to the class on Friday. "It is a great loss for them and a great loss for the school." Her squeaky voice shakes, and I look down at my desk, the desk that I had chosen for the school year because Sarah had sat in it four years before and had carved her name in it with a compass point. In the silent minute that follows, I trace the letters of her name over and over again. Sarah Iris, carved deep in its wooden face.

"My desk is a tombstone," I think. "My desk is my sister's tombstone." Then I place my head down on it and let my tears fill up the grooves of her name.

Father comes home late. He drops his briefcase quietly on the floor and buries his hands deep in his pockets. He looks at Mother and me, sitting but not talking, facing each other like two mannequins in opposite store windows.

"I spent most of the day at Lakeside Police Station." Father says. "They haven't been found in the Cape. Sergeant Grobbler said they could be as far as Bulawayo or even as far north as Nairobi in their camping trailer by now. Said the police didn't have the time to start tracking down a bunch of gypsy wanderers."

"But she's dead." Mother's voice quivers.

"Lily, there's nothing we can do, nothing we can do at all." Father says wearily.

Mother lowers her eyes and runs her hand nervously back and forth on the couch. "Tell Emily, Bob." Mother looks up at me, her face waxy white.

"Emily." Father clears his throat, starts to sit down on the couch next to Mother, then changes his mind and paces around the coffee table. "We decided last night. It's no good for us to be here anymore. No good at all. We need to move away from this house . . . the lake, too many memories . . ."

As he speaks I see my world thrown, like playing cards, into the air. Snuggling with Sarah in her bed, playing checkers with her on the lawn, Lettie making *pap* and *mielie meal* in the kitchen, No-Name curled asleep in a corner of my Cattery Club, the white pillars and the jacaranda trees, the woods and the sun streaming through the trees, the gravel on the driveway . . . and Buza. Buza at the gates, Buza on his stool, Buza's snuffbox and his *muthi* tins.

"What will happen to Buza if we move, Father?"

"I'll give him an excellent reference." Father clears his throat again. "We won't need a night watchman. I'm not expecting that we'll live opposite a wood again."

"Mother!" I cry, "Buza's been with you since you were young! You can't just let him go! Please!" I fall on my knees in front of her.

"Lettie will come with us. We need to move, Emily." Mother looks pleadingly at me.

I run to Father, pound my fists against his chest with all my strength. "Go! You go! I'm going with him. I don't care, I'd rather be with Buza!"

Father holds my aching fists still, pulls me toward him, holds me tight against his creased white shirt. "Please, Emily," he whispers into my hair, "we need you, you're our only— We need to be a family."

"It's too late!" I spit out at him. "Ask her." I point at Mother accusingly. "Ask her if we're a family! Well, Mother, are we? Are we?"

Mother stands slowly. Steadies herself with one hand on the edge of the couch. She looks straight into my eyes, and I feel her tearful gaze reach deep inside me. She holds out her hand to me. "Please, Emily," she says, "Emily," her fingers reaching and reaching for me.

"Answer the question, Mother," I whisper. A moment of white silence slices through the air.

"Dear God, Emily, what do you want from me?"

I watch Mother's fingers as they shimmer in front of me and hear Buza's words swirling inside my head. *For me, the stars in Zululand, they are a little brighter. But maybe is because my family is there.*

"Father," I say without taking my eyes from Mother's hand,

"Buza has a daughter in Zululand. Send him home, Father, so he can be with his daughter."

"Money, Emily, what'll he do for money? The man needs to work." Father moves beside Mother, whose hand still hovers midair.

"Give it to him, Bob." Mother holds my gaze. "Emily, is that what you want?" Mother's green eyes spill over. "Buza's been with us for years. Give him a pension. Take the money from your chocolate business, Bob. I don't care. God knows the man deserves it." She holds both hands out toward me. "See, Emily? I'm trying," she cries.

I go to her, fall against her, hold her softness, feel her warmth against my skin. Here is Mother cradling me, holding me.

"Mommy," I cry, "Mommy!"

But it is me who steps away. Me, who untangles myself from her embrace, leaving her with outstretched empty arms.

7 Zululand

"It is a long journey, Miss Emily, but a very beautiful one. Maybe you will take it someday." Buza sits on his wooden stool at the bottom of the gates with me for the last time.

"Tell me, Buza, tell me."

The late afternoon sun catches the tops of the white pillars, and they glow like burning torches against the rosy sky. I feel the grass, softer than before, under me, the gravel stones, sharper as I roll them in my hands, and the sound of Buza's voice, stronger and more soothing to my ears than ever. I think how sometimes before things are taken away, they get clearer, bigger, like they've been put under a magnifying glass for you to look at extra closely for the last time.

"Nearly two days, it takes, first the train, then the bus." Buza runs an oil rag over his new stick, polishing it for his journey back home. "Me, I don't look out the window too much until we cross the Drakensberg Mountains." He holds out his hand and draws the mountains with his fingertip against the sunset. "You see them, Miss Emily, sharp, purple points, like the back of a dragon. We call them Quathlamba. It means the "barrier of spears." Behind them, the Maluti Mountains of Basutoland. Ah, they are something to see, Miss Emily, something to see." Buza's eyes shine, then he looks at me, sees the longing in my face to be beside him on the train. "Come, close your eyes, Miss Emily," he says softly, and places his finger on my forehead. "I will take you with me across the Tugela River to Zululand."

He takes me in the warm breeze of the late spring evening, from our gates, from the suburbs of Johannesburg to a place where I can hear the shrill cry of a *uCilo* bird as it makes its way across the matted *kloofs* of Nongoma; where I can see the crumpled green hills of Ulundi that are covered with *kraals;* the Zulu huts that sprout across the land like patches of mushrooms; the black silhouettes of herd boys sitting like small tree stumps, watching their cattle in the wiry shade of thorn trees in the valley of the Black Umfolozi River.

"Here, Miss Emily," Buza says, his voice coming deep and proud from inside him, "this is where my home is."

He takes my hand in his, and I open my eyes. We watch the sun as it races away from us, watch the woods grow dark and still.

"I will think often of you, Miss Emily," he says, as night comes quickly around us holding Buza and me in its velvet blanket together for the last time.

Johannesburg Station. Two carved stone heads of African elephant bulls with gigantic tusks hang above the entrance.

"So big and strong but so gentle," Buza looks up at them as

we pass under them into the station and make our way to the track he is to leave from.

When we get to his train we have to stand across from each other, separated by a platform barrier. Father and I on one side, Buza on the other. WHITES ONLY / NET BLANKES is written in big letters on the side of the train that we stand next to. NON-WHITES / NIE BLANKES on the side where Buza stands.

He wears his old green coat and carries a tattered brown suitcase and a taped-up cardboard box that has his *muthi* tins and blankets inside it. Around us is the noise of the station, voices yelling good-bye, luggage being loaded, the sharp screech of train wheels grinding against tracks.

Behind Buza are black faces, Basuto blankets, lumpy bundles being squeezed into the tail end of the train, while behind us, buttoned-up whites in well-cut coats, with neat suitcases and unscuffed baggage, file easily into the largest part of the train.

"Well, then." Father reaches for Buza's hand across the low wooden barrier and gives his hand a firm shake. "Good luck, old man."

"Baas Bob," Buza looks Father warmly in the eye, "Thank you, I thank you for the money. I thank you many times over." He lowers his head and places his hands together, his new stick clasped between his palms.

"Emily," Father turns to me, "Buza needs to start getting onto the train." He points to the barrier. "We can't cross over this to help him with his belongings. You need to say good-bye now, Emily."

"Like the Drakensberg Mountains," Buza says softly and looks across the wooden rail that separates us. "Barrier of spears."

I run my hand along the sharp surface and reach for him across it, feel the wooden planks between us press into my body, like purple points.

"Don't cry, Miss Emily." Buza holds me tightly. "Don't cry."

He lets go of me and takes my face in his hands. Then crouches down so that his face is close and level with mine, the barrier between us, like a picture frame, surrounding his face. The deep riverbed wrinkles, his feathery gray eyelashes, the mist clouding his muddy old eyes. I stamp Buza inside my head forever.

"I never tell you, Miss Emily, what the word Zulu mean. I tell you now." His gentle voice rumbles in his throat.

"What does it mean, Buza?" I cry, still clutching on to his coat.

"It mean 'heaven's people.' And it is you, Miss Emily, you who has made it possible for me to return to my heaven, my Zululand." He grips both my hands, pulls them free from his pockets, and as he releases them I feel his warm tears spill onto the tops of my hands, like the last drops of honey-glue.

Moving

On the final day, I sit in my Cattery Club with Duna, Coco, and No-Name.

"We'll build another Cattery Club at the new house, Emily. There's enough space." Father had put his head in earlier, when he brought a cardboard box for my cat statues and pictures to be packed into. But I told him no, it wouldn't be the same.

Yesterday, Mother took Lettie and me to the new house to drop off a few things. It's a half-hour drive away in the freshly built-up suburb of Sandown. White walls and big empty rooms. A neat front lawn. No room for the chickens anymore.

"The cats will have to stay indoors until they get used to it here," Mother said in her wispy new voice as we walked quietly through the hollow house.

"They won't like being locked up. How long will it take, Mother, before they get used to it?"

"I don't know, Emily." She ran a hand across her unmade eyes. "I just don't know."

I walk for the last time to the servants' quarters. To Buza's room, where his iron bed still stands on bricks. His comforting smell is soaked into the air, and it seeps inside me. I say his name out loud in the empty space and imagine him in Zululand, sitting on his wooden stool, his back to the rolling Umfolozi hills. Matilda's son sits on his knee, looking up at him with big, dark eyes as Buza tells him a story of proud Zulu warriors from long ago.

I reach for the scrap of paper inside my shorts pocket, the only piece of Buza that's left for me to hold on to. "It is a P.O. box, Miss Emily. You write me there, you write to me. Matilda, she read English good. She will read your letters to me," Buza had said, giving me the paper as we first entered the train station.

Now, I feel it crumpled against my palm, calming me, as if it were Buza's wrinkled fingers I'm holding in my pocket. I close his door and wander back through our half-empty house.

The late afternoon sun casts wide shadows over the movers and their vans and the stacked boxes in the driveway. I watch the men from the veranda. Strangers loading up our lives, carrying away bits of Sarah. Her clothes and belongings stand in a separate pile, going to an orphanage with "To Be Delivered" written across their closed box flaps. "It's good that needy children are getting my things, Emily," I imagine Sarah's gentle voice saying to me.

The white pillars at the bottom of the driveway shimmer, and I feel myself pulled toward them, wanting to lean against them one last time. Here, I think, here was where I sat at his feet. Here is where I listened. Here is where I learned.

I was named after Buza, the teacher of the mighty King Shaka, I hear Buza telling Streak and me.

Through the woods I wander. I pick up shavings of blue gum bark and fill my pockets with them. I will paste them in a book, I think, and keep them forever, so that when I stand and look out across the road of the new house and see the walls and windows of the houses across the street, I will have the woods with me. I will take the trees with me because tomorrow there will be no winding bends, no smell of blue gum trees, no distant sound of a buffalo in the night. Without my sister, Sarah. Without Buza. Living in a new house where, Mother says, there will be no room for guests to come and stay anymore.

When I reach the lake, I feel the weight of its water inside my chest. Green and thick and murky. A hidden demon that took my sister. At the water's edge, near the shack, is the same boatman, chaining the chipped rowboats to the dock for the night. He looks up, sees me standing, my pockets bulging with blue gum strips, my feet kicking at nothing on the ground.

"*Meisie*, girl, come," he curls a fat finger out toward me.

I fix my eyes on the fountain in the middle of the water, think about the fountain lights going on in their cotton candy bright colors and wonder about the dwarf-man who might live inside it. A last chance, I think, to row out to the middle of the lake and reach the fountain when the lights go on.

"*Meisie, kom,* I want to tell you something." The boatman waves his floppy arm toward me. There, bouncing against his flabby middle like the unsteady boats chained to the dock, are the keys to the rowboats. I walk slowly toward him, wondering if just once he might let a boat out onto the lake after closing time.

The boatman stands in front of the shack, a half-eaten cheese sandwich caught between his rubbery lips.

I move close to the boats at the water's edge, not wanting to be any nearer to him, yet wanting badly to ask the favor of him.

"Youse want some?" he says, reaching into his soiled overall pocket and pulling out the other half of his sandwich.

"No, thank you," I say, trying hard not to look into his bloated face.

"I remember you." He throws the rest of his sandwich toward a flock of geese, who hiss loudly and fight over the scraps. Then he wipes his thick fingers down the front of his overalls. "Youse was on the lake with those two scruffy boys not so long ago, and the pretty girl with the long red hair, no?"

"Yes," I whisper. "My sister."

"Your sister." The boatman pauses, then shakes his head. "Hellova shame." He pinches the sides of his veiny nose with two fingers. "Didn't know she was your sister. Youse don't look nothing like her."

Another group of geese waddle over and stand hissing between us.

"*Weg, weg!* No more bread." He shoos them away. "No more."

As the geese scatter, the boatman takes a step toward me. "I recognized her, see. All that red hair, so pretty. Not many *meisies* have hair like that. . . . I was just starting to pull the boats out from the shack for the day. Thought it was a bit odd that she was out at the lake so early in the morning, and alone. Yelled out to her to be careful when I saw her wading in. She waved and smiled. Then I went back into the shack to get the next boat when I hear a cry for help. Knew right away she was in too deep when I ran out. Rowed as fast as I could. She tried hard to stay afloat, but then she disappeared under the water. I kept hollerin' and hollerin', '*Meisie! Meisie!*' "

I cover my mouth and let out a sob.

"I jumped into the water then, swam like there was no tomorrow all over the lake. Finally felt her underneath the thick weeds. Pulled her out, I did, but I got to her too late. . . ." His voice trails off.

"Sarah wasn't feeling well. Wasn't thinking how dangerous . . ."

"Youse must know how much I wanted to save her." He looks at me with blotchy red eyes. "Terrible, it was. Haven't been able to sleep much since. . . ." The boatman lowers his head. "I just want to say I'm sorry about your sister. Very sorry, miss."

A hard breeze comes across the water, blows into my stinging eyes. I think about the boatman's hands on Sarah, dragging her from the water, remember how Sarah had pulled away fast from him when he had rolled the oar toward her across the countertop and made her spill the bread crumbs onto the ground.

"Sarah didn't like people being rough with her." I manage to get past the ache in my throat. "She didn't like roughness at all."

"Miss, I was very careful with your sister. Laid her down right here." He points to a place on the cracked cement dock.

"Covered her with a canvas boat cover when I knew. . . . Well, you know, still, I called for an ambulance, just in case. When they got here I pointed them through the woods to those white pillars. Must have sent someone up there while the others worked on her, tried to get the water outta her. . . ." He waves in the direction of our house through the distant trees. "I remembered, see, where she lived. Like I said, not too many girls with hair as pretty as hers. Never forget hair like that." The boatman looks at me square in the face, shakes his head again, then turns to go back to the shack.

Thoughts flow fast through me, flood my head. Sarah, wanting to feel better. Sarah wanting to be perfect and neat again. Sarah wanting to wash all the ugliness away in the lake water.

"Wait, sir, *meneer.*" I walk quickly to catch up with him. "Please, I have a favor to ask."

"What is it, *meisie?*"

"My family, we're moving away tomorrow. I wondered if you would let me, if I could go out on the lake to the fountain one last time?"

The boatman frowns, clucks his tongue against his teeth. "After hours, miss. Not supposed to let nobody on the lake after six."

"Please, just this once," I ask.

He puts his hands on his hips, rocks back and forth on his heels. "Look," he says, "I can't let you go out alone, but you can come with me, if you like. I have to row out to the fountain myself now. Okay, *meisie?*"

"Okay," I say, my heart pounding against my insides. "Did they ever catch him?" I ask, as the boatman begins to unlock the chain that holds the boats secure to the dock.

"Who, *meisie*, who?"

"The man who cut the woman's body up and left it in the lake?"

The boatman lets out a rough laugh. "Oh, *ja*, they caught him all right. In Beaufort West in the Cape. Found him doing the same thing there. Fishermen pulling up plastic bags, just the same." He looks up at me from his crouched position, then stands, coughing and out of breath. "Youse was worried, *meisie?* Thought maybe it was me?" He laughs again. "Hell, I know I'm not a pretty sight, but fish is about the only thing I've ever thrown back into a lake."

"I'm sorry . . . I didn't mean . . ."

"No worry, *meisie*. You just lost your sister, and moving and everything." He scratches his bristly chin and looks over at me, "In Afrikaans we say, *Alles moet verbygaan*—everything will pass. But still it must be hard on one so young."

"Twelve," I say. "I'm twelve, and my name's Emily."

"Willem," the boatman puts out his chapped hand to me, and I shake it. "*Kom*, Emily, get in." He steadies the unfastened gray boat, and I climb over the middle seat and make my way to the back while Willem sits in the center and rows us out across the lake, whistling a tune between his rubbery lips.

I watch the weeping willow trees on the lake's edge, their stringy green branches dipping into the water, as if bowing to it.

I imagine Sarah's spirit under the water, floating among the fish and the stones, laughing at the missing hand of the woman dancing as it conducts a school of fish beneath the water. I don't hear Willem; it is only Sarah's voice that comes to me through the murky water, her words rolling toward me through the slapping of the oars as they cut below the surface. "Live and be strong. Inside yourself you will find great strength. There you will find me."

"Here we are, *meisie*." The smacking sound of the oars, as the boatman pulls them in, jolts me back. We slide under the fountain, the spray sprinkling our clothes, then the boat bumps against the diamond-shaped base of the fountain.

I look out from inside the falling stream of water, see a reddish glow highlighting the tops of the trees, the feathers on the backs of the geese that float by, the rolling ripples on the lake. A brilliant tangerine color that's spilled over everything, like the color of Sarah's hair.

It is in this moment that I find my own tale to send Buza for all the ones he has given me. I will write to him and tell him that it is Sarah's beautiful red hair that has kissed everything here. Sarah's goodness that covers the lake with her glowing light. "This story," Buza will tell his grandson, his stick at his side, "Is how Sarah's goodness and beautiful red hair makes the sunset over Zebra Lake." Then it will be passed down so that Sarah can live on forever in the voices of storytellers.

Willem shakes my arm. "Miss, miss, you're daydreaming," he says gently. "Have to switch on the colored lights. See the switch right here." The boatman opens a metal flap. "These bulbs, they go all around here at the base." He points to the rows of pink, green, and blue bulbs that run like beads around the fountain base. "They's what make the fountain change color at night, you see." He smiles at me. "One of my jobs is to light the fountain. Makes me happy every time I switch them on. Hey, why don't you do it this time? Might cheer you up a bit." He points his finger at the light switch.

"Buza, our old night watchman, he said that I could make magic happen," I say proudly.

"Go on, then." Willem chuckles. "Make magic, *meisie!*" He opens his arms wide to the sky as I throw the switch. "Beautiful, just beautiful." He looks up at the shimmering blue spray, which falls like a thousand shooting stars onto the water.

"Please. Let me go right under it!"

"No problems, little miss, no problems." He turns my side of the boat with his oar into the spray. Brilliant blue water soaks my hair, seeps into my ears, floods my eyelashes, spills over me, washes into me.

And through the brilliant blue that showers down on me, I shout out loud, "See, Sarah, there really is a dwarf-man. All the time I knew there was a dwarf-man!" I laugh so hard, with my mouth open to the colored spray until it fills my mouth with its sweet, good taste, and from behind the rush of the water I can hear the boatman saying, "Emily, little miss, are you okay, are you okay?"

But my laughter and the taste of the pink bubblegum spray as the lights change color, and the saltiness of my own tears fill my mouth so that I cannot answer, cannot tell him that, yes, I am all right. I am all right.

Epilogue

There is a road that runs north through the Phabeni River Valley, an etched covering of dust that winds its way lazily over great mountains toward the Sabi River.

High above the valley, on a windy hilltop, where orange groves glow golden in graceful rows on each rise and their lush fragrance scents the air, stands a modest house. Deep purple bougainvillea cling to its mellowed walls, their buds traveling freely under the open veranda trellis.

Beyond the white-painted trellis, a lone baobab tree faces the escarpment, its gigantic trunk darkening with the late afternoon mist that hangs over the valley.

If you come upon this part of the lowveld as the sun goes down, you will be humbled by the stillness of the mountains, enchanted by the sweetness in the air, and you will know that you have entered one of the loveliest valleys in the eastern Transvaal. It is called Manungi, nestled on the road between White River and Hazyview. Here, in the gentle folds of this valley, I have made my home.

I am a grown woman now, living far from the man-made

gold mountains of Johannesburg, of my childhood. My husband and I own a small restaurant on the outskirts of White River. Red-shuttered, jolly, and crowded, with the smell of garlic and good pasta sauce wafting over the local farms, La Bella Fontana, the beautiful fountain, has become as indigenous to the farmlands as the orange groves that surround it.

On weekends I work in the restaurant, pouring Cape Zinfandel and Nederburg wines from carafes, straightening checkered tablecloths and chatting with the locals. But during the week, I am usually at home in the garden with my easel and paints, trying to capture on canvas the extraordinary beauty of water, mist, and mountains. Sometimes I venture out to Bridal Veil or to the Sabi Falls, where the Sabi River flows slow and placid between shady banks, only to crash suddenly over sheer cliffs, making rainbows dance in a fine flung spray. I have tried to capture the frozen moment when the serene water suddenly plummets in an unexpected explosive torrent over the sheer cliff. But those moments remain elusive, much as they are in life.

I sit today on the veranda of our home with a sketchpad on my knees. With broad pastel strokes I smudge deep scarlet and vibrant yellow together across the empty whiteness of the page.

My daughter. It is her red hair, caught against the brilliance of the oranges that are full and ripe on the green trees, that I try to re-create. The blending together of her and the trees, the trees and her. She will, I think, remember orange trees as her special childhood trees, just as blue gums are mine.

I watch her, this small child of mine, as she sings and skips through the grove in her pretty blue dress, disturbing a noisy group of glossy starlings as she goes. A tightening in my throat, with the memory of how the late afternoon sun would catch Sarah's hair just so.

"Mommy, is it time, is it time yet?" her sweet voice calls across the lawn.

"Not yet," I call back, "just a few more minutes." I tell her there is a letter and package that I need to open first and that she should go and fetch the basket in the meantime.

She runs toward me, her hair a shining halo in flight, the sun closing down fast on the familiar mountains behind her. She scampers past me, smearing a quick kiss on my face, leaving her sweet breath lingering on my cheeks. Then I reach for the package at my feet. The package from Buza.

I like to open his letters at sunset, for it is in the brooding quiet of dusk that he is most with me.

Today arrived both a letter and a package from him. He is in his nineties now, his eyesight gone, his legs no longer able to hold him up even with the help of his trusted stick. His grandson, Ezekiel, has taken over the role of letter writer for Buza since his daughter Matilda's promotion to head nurse at Nongoma Mission Hospital. But they are Buza's words that have reached me all these years, no matter whose handwriting they may have been inked in.

I run my fingers over the clean white envelope, touch the stamp of a male Kudu in the right-hand corner, and open the letter.

Sakubona, Miss Emily.

My grandson, Ezekiel, who is sitting beside my bed,
says that I must rest, but I told him not until I write
this letter to you. Ezekiel, he is soon beginning with
his studies to become a lawyer. Did I tell you this in
my last letter? He laughs at me when I say to him
that he will use a pen to fight instead of a spear. He,
like Mr. Mandela, will be one of the new warriors in
Africa. I am happy to be alive for this great honor. To
have one of my own who is willing to shake the branch
of a tree.

Although I do not see anymore, I still see you in my
head, like you were when I worked for Baas Bob and
Madam Lily, and how you looked when you visited me
two summers ago here in Zululand after the death
of your own father. It saddens me still to think that
even after Miss Sarah's passing your Mother and
Father could not find a way to be together. Perhaps
it was better that their paths did not stay as one.
Me, I must believe there was not enough honey-glue
between them.

Soon, I am feeling, I will go to meet the great
uNkulunkulu. I will tell Miss Sarah, when I meet her
there, that you are a fine woman now. Strong and
gentle like the stone elephants outside the Johannesburg train station. I remember the day I left so very
well. I thought my soul would break to say good-bye
to you.

Miss Emily, Ezekiel says I must rest, but it is this I must say to you. For me, in this life, I have two daughters. Matilda and you, Miss Emily.

I have sent to you something very special. You will know when you open it.

Sala kahle, my daughter, God Bless.

Buza.

I hold the letter in my hands, his words, as beautiful as the dazzling wings of a lilac-breasted roller in flight, hidden against its feathery chest and magically revealed as it soars, dark-lilac and blue.

A chacma baboon swings noisily through the grove, picks an orange, and braces its bared yellow teeth around the skin. For a moment I think of Otis, his yellowed teeth, how I remember him the first day in the camping trailer. He must be a man by now. Must be. And Streak? Probably on the road, I think, somewhere free and wild, a guitar slung over his back, never settling in one place for too long. Not knowing where to look for the kind of life he was never given. But none of this I really know.

I open Buza's package, small and well bound. My fingers unsteady on the tape, peeling it open gently, as if the paper were his fragile skin. And then it is there in my hand, perfect in its symmetry, whole and complete, the remaining light catching its flawless shell. It is an egg, the small white egg of a honeyguide bird.

I look out across the escarpment, hold the egg close against my chest, feel its wholeness against my own.

I think of Sarah, her marmalade smell, the comfort of her bed; of Streak in his "school uniform," his needy eyes for the kitten he never got to have; of Buza, his guiding, gentle hands painting tales against the background of the blue gums.

And then it comes to me, how Streak was wrong. Things with names don't go away. They live on forever. Their souls woven into the fabric of our beings; their magic dusted across our memories; their stories, our folktales to tell forever. Yes, I will keep them all with me, not just the fragments, the scattered pieces. They will live with me always, whole and complete. Buza, Sarah, Streak.

"Mommy, is it time?" My daughter comes toward me, the basket of kittens mewing in her hands.

"Yes, it's time for the Sunset Naming Ceremony," I say.

She hands the striped tabby to me. I roll the kitten gently in my hands, feel it soft and warm against my skin.

"This one," I say, looking into its wise, brown eyes, "we will name after a great warrior." I place my child's palms gently beneath mine on the kitten. "This one, my little Sarafina, we will call Buza."

Acknowledgments

I am blessed to have been supported by a group of remarkable people who never wavered in their belief that this story would find the perfect publishing home. I am forever grateful to writing teacher and author Barbara Abercrombie, who encouraged me, all those years ago, to take my short story named "Gypsies" and expand it into a novel. To my beautiful and very best friend, Kathy Jackoway, who dusted off the manuscript and put it in the hands of Leigh Taylor Young, the spirit and gentle force who helped this novel find its way to Alicia Gordon at the William Morris Agency. My utmost appreciation to her for passing it on to her East Coast colleague, Jonathan Pecarsky, my splendid agent who must be especially thanked for his endurance and faith in me. I am hugely indebted to Kate Farrell, my wonderful editor at Henry Holt and Company, whose astute guiding hand has made the experience of being edited both edifying and enjoyable. Kate's passion and belief in this book has been nothing short of astounding. Many thanks to Holt copyeditor Ana Deboo and Senior Production Editor Marianne Cohen, for their many hours of meticulous work on my manuscript. Also thanks to Susan Hawk, Director of Marketing at Henry Holt.

I am also deeply grateful to my older sister, Caron, the calming voice of reason in my life, and my mother, Ruth, who is always there in moments of need. A special thanks to Dr. Ron Furst for his generosity and years of genuinely caring about me. A big hug goes to niece Lori and nephew Danny; sister Nicky; Doug and nephew Bennett Meyer; author and writing teacher Lisa Lieberman Doctor, my great support in all that I write; and Damon Shalit, who shares my nostalgia and love for the country of our birth.

Thanks to long-time friends Barbara Mandel, Sharon Cicero, Charlotte Booth, Patty Wheelock, Ceslie Armstrong, and Andrea Kerzner: You lovely women mean the world to me. A word of appreciation to ex-husband, Marvin Katz, who is a constant in my life and who still manages to make me laugh. My gratitude to my other family—Ronnie Katz, Vickie and Rod Espudo, and baby Emma J.—for their love and support.

An extra word of thanks to my one-in-a-million father, Harold, who taught me to relish good literature and whose input and knowledge added so much to this book. There are no words to truly describe my love and gratitude to him. Thank you, my lovely daughter Jordan, for being the supreme individual that you are—you are my greatest joy. Lastly, this book honors the late Nellie Letlape and all the black women and men of South Africa who gave tirelessly and unselfishly of themselves to us, the privileged white children of South Africa, during the harsh era of Apartheid. We can never repay them for all that they did for us.

Sala kahle!

Glossary

Afrikaans Words and Expressions

Apartheid. The racist doctrine of "separate development." Black people in South Africa were labeled as second-class citizens and discriminated against in every area of life. In 1994 apartheid officially came to an end and the first democratic elections were held in South Africa, with people of all races being able to vote. A government of national unity was formed, with Nelson Rolihlahla Mandela as president.

Baas. Master.

Biltong. Meat cut in strips, slightly salted, and dried in the open air.

Bliksem. Scoundrel.

Braai. Barbecue.

Dagga. Marijuana.

Doek. Head scarf.

Ja. Yes.

Julle hoor. You hear (plural).

Kaffir. A derogatory term for a black person.

Kloof. A gorge, ravine.

Knobkerrie. A wooden staff with a rounded knobbly top.

Kom. Come.

Kraal. A number of dwelling huts together under the head of the family.

Maak gou! Be quick! Move it!

Melktert. Custard pie.

Meisie. Girl.

Meneer. Mister.

Mielie meal. Corn porridge.

Pap. Sticky white porridge made from corn.

Riempie. Narrow softened rawhide used for caning the backs and seats of chairs.

Skelm. A rascal.

Weg! weg! Go! go! Scram! Beat it!

Zulu Words and Expressions

Abathakathi. Wizard who uses power for evil purposes.

Amakhubalo. Medicinal roots.

Assegai. Stabbing or hunting spear.

Ayzirorie! Exclamation.

Ayziwena! Exclamation.

Buza (BOO-zah). His name means "ask a question."

Dingiswayo. Wanderer; outcast.

Hai! Exclamation.

Hau! Exclamation.

Hai wena! Good gracious!

Hayakona! No! Never!

iBonsi. Shrub with fruit like an apricot.

iGoli. "The Golden One"—Johannesburg.

Indaba. A meeting to discuss matters, a parley; colloquially, a problem, or to sort out a problem.

inDuna. Zulu name for a state official appointed by the king or by a local chief. (Duna is the name of one of Emily's cats.)

i-Nsedhlu bird. Honeyguide bird; guides animals and humans to bees' nests.

Inteleze. War medicine.

Isibindi. Courage.

isiCoco. Headring worn by a married Zulu. (Coco is the name of one of Emily's cats.)

Izinswelaboya. Wizards who use parts of the human body to carry out their evil works.

Kunjalo. It is said.

Mnta-na-mi. My child.

Muthi. Herbal medicines.

Nkosi sikelel' iAfrika. The anthem ("God Bless Africa") of the African National Congress (ANC), a group that would become the first majority black political party to lead the country. Since 1997, the South African national anthem became a hybrid song combining the verses from "Nkosi sikelel' iAfrika" and verses from the former national anthem of South Africa, "Die Stem van Suid-Afrika."

Quathlamba. "Barrier of Spears"—The Drakensberg Mountains.

Sakubona (also **Sawubona**). Greetings; good day; hello.

Sala kahle! Stay well; adieu; farewell.

Shaka. King of the Zulus at the height of their military power, from 1816 to 1828. He was a fierce and militaristic ruler, an inventive military commander, and an astute political survivor. In the early nineteenth century he created the most powerful kingdom in southern Africa.

Silo Sikazulu! King of the Zulus!

Sina. Dancing in general.

Tokalosh. A wicked elfish man, like an evil leprechaun.

Tsotsie. Colloquially, young delinquent; street thug.

Ukubonga. Thanksgiving sacrifice of praise when something good has come about.

Ukuthetha. A sacrifice when things are going badly, to find out what the people have done wrong to be so persecuted by their ancestors.

Umfaan. Boy.

Um-liliwane. A little fire; a term of endearment.

Umthakathi. A witch, wizard, warlock who uses his/her powers for antisocial ends.

umThala. The Milky Way.

uNkulunkulu. God; the Creator; the First Cause.

Xhosa. The Xhosa people in South Africa number approximately 8 million. Xhosa is a Nguni language, a subgroup that also includes Zulu. The sounds of Xhosa, and even the name Xhosa, begins with a click of the tongue. Xhosa is one of eleven official languages spoken in South Africa.

Zulu. The Zulu people are an African ethnic group of about 11 million people who live mainly in KwaZulu-Natal Province, South Africa. This area is one of the most beautiful in the country, with the sea, rolling green mountains, and natural forests in valleys.